DC Homicide

Tyler Craig

Prince Harles Publishing

Contents

Three victims.

One white female, two black men.

They looked good strung up to the warehouse pillars, the killer thought. It had been easier than anticipated. Their fearful faces were contorted with sweat and pain.

The advance was slow, hands clenched into fists. The strikes were relentless and furious, and the prisoners were left beaten to a pulp.

"You thought you could just ruin my family—ruin my whole life—and get away with it, didn't you?"

Gunfire rant out. Eight shots in all.

"But you were wrong," the solemn voice spoke into the silence. "You were dead wrong."

A single victim remained, muffled screams dissipating into pitiful whimpers as he accepted his fate.

"Don't you worry my dear...I'll be back for you."

The laughter receded as the killer walked down the hall, leaving the third victim alive. This wasn't just any old murder—it was the perfect crime. There was much work to be done.

Chapter One

"Denver! Barnaby!" The desk sergeant yelled. "We got a professional skirt who ate a breakfast of lead over in the FT! Grab your keys and head out. I'll pass along the directions over the radio as soon as I get them." I stood up, nodded at my partner, and headed right out the door.

I'm Max Denver. Jack Barnaby is my partner. We work Homicide for the Metropolitan Police Department in Washington D.C. It was our first call of the day. Lucky for us, this particular crime scene was close to the precinct.

By the time Jack and I had gotten to the scene, the chalk fairy had already left her mark on the cement and released the body to the coroner. She left a bold two inch white limestone outline around the body, which showed us exactly where the dead dame was found–about three feet from an alley dumpster, seven feet from the main drag.

This part of town used to be called Murder Bay by the locals, which was pretty fitting at that time. The government shut that down once they started building up all these fancy new facilities to house books and feds and whatnot–can't have a neighborhood with a name like that this close to the White House. Not in 1950, at least.

The Federal Triangle is what they call it now, but this used to be the place to go if you were looking for some company. Back then, these streets were lined with whore houses throughout the entire neighborhood. That was a bit before my time, but Jack told me some stories. He's been on the force for close to fifty years now, and he's seen a thing or two.

Now they were blowing the poles of the pols, if you catch my drift. Men in fancy suits with bigger salaries. Johns who had their own cars. No more ducking behind a dumpster in an alley to earn a buck. No, today's working girls had it easy compared to those of the Prohibition Era. And from what we were hearing, the bird who was laying there on the sidewalk an hour ago was most definitely a woman of the night.

The thing with cases like these was it was almost impossible to get a proper ID of the victims. Even when we did get a name, it was usually a stage name like Dreamy, or Starla, or something crazy like that. Not once did we ever come across a Nancy or a Sue or an Ann.

"Whatcha think, Maxey?" Jack asked as we were hovering over the outline like a pair of seagulls flying circles over a picnic.

"Working girl, that's about all I gots right now," I replied. "Who found the body?"

"Some kids. They was playing stickball in the alley when the ball rolled over here. Kid went to retrieve the ball and found the dead broad instead."

"Poor kid," I said. I couldn't imagine finding a dead body at that age. Especially not in a place where I played stickball. I didn't sleep for over a month after I saw my first body on the job.

"I wouldn't want to be that kid's mother, I'll tell you that much right now," I said to Jack as we looked around the scene.

"No kidding. Wonder why this world keeps breeding scumbags when the purity of the youth keeps getting lost earlier and earlier. A real head scratcher, ain't it? Not the way I'd want to lose my innocence," Jack replied.

"Got that right, Jackie Boy," I returned. "You ask Davis if he got an address for that kid? We're gonna need to talk to him ourselves. Can't rely on these jerks for anything," I laughed. I could count on one hand the times that we actually got an address from the first coppers on the scene.

"Nope. Go figure," he said. Jack was always the one to gather all the information from the cops who were on the scene first while I looked the area over to see if I could spot some fresh evidence. That's how it was on the first day we had worked together, and it's been that way ever since.

"Well, whatcha say we go pay them kids a visit, then? Give 'em something to tell their friends tomorrow on the schoolyard," I said to Jack as I started back to our car.

Jack nodded. "You got it, Maxey," he said. "Let's go."

Chapter Two

J ack and I had a certain way of doing things. Whenever we would approach a house, I would get out and knock on the door while Jack would stay back so he could keep a lookout–make sure nobody took off running out the back. I'd much rather have him at the front door with me. But I'm the one who drew the short stick back on my first day, so I get to do the knocking. No matter if it's questioning a witness, or telling a family member that their loved one wasn't going to make it home for supper that night, I got to do the heavy lifting. Jack always told me it was because I had sympathetic eyes, but I think maybe he just liked to watch me squirm under the pressure.

"Hi, ma'am," I tipped my hat and flashed my tin to the lady who answered the door. This was still a heavily colored part of town, so it was no surprise to see a black woman open the door. She looked to be heavyset, in her mid-thirties, with bags under her eyes. *We definitely have the right house*, I thought to myself. I tried my best to get a peek at the interior of the house behind her, but if I'm honest, she took up most of the door frame. The only items I saw behind her were a pair of scruffy work boots, a family photo from a nearby campground, and an old black cane resting against the coat rack next to the front door.

"I'm detective Denver with Metro PD. My partner and I were as-signed the case for the woman that was found in the alley this afternoon. We were told that the kids who found her might live here. Is that true?"

"Yes, thank you for coming. My boys have been scared to death ever since they came home, and I don't know what to do. My husband is away right now, and I don't know how to tell them everything is gonna be alright–they're just kids. They shouldn't have to see something like that. This scared them pretty good," she said, as I saw tears start to well up in her eyes.

"They always play ball out in that alley on the weekends," she continued, "and I've seen girls like that strolling by, eyeballing those boys, even talking to them sometimes. I know this isn't the nicest part of town, but I never thought we'd see something like that so close to home. It's just not right." She looked at me as she almost broke down, but managed to stay strong for her children's sake.

"I agree, ma'am. Things are better around here than what they used to be, but crime doesn't seem to have any borders anymore. Hell, last week we caught a body right behind the White House. You'd think that would be sacred grounds, but these dirtbags just don't seem to care anymore."

The alarm in her eyes made me realize I had said too much. I would have to be less loose-lipped if I was going to get a chance to question those kids.

"Any chance I could speak to your boys? We don't have much down at the crime scene to go off of, and any help they could offer us would be appreciated. It won't take long. I just have a few questions for them."

Despite her hesitance, she nodded. "Is it okay if I stay with them while you talk? They're already having a rough time. I don't want them to get any more scared than they already are,"

"Of course, Ma'am. I'm going to get my partner from the car while you round up the kids. His name is Detective Barnaby. He may look old and mean, but he's as cuddly as a teddy bear, I promise," I said with a smile. That last part was a lie, but one that I hoped would put her more at ease.

"Yes. Yes, of course. I'll be right back with the boys."

As soon as she closed her front door, I turned towards the car and gave Jack a wave, motioning him up onto the porch with me.

"What'd she say?" He asked, which made me roll my eyes at him. He'd have known if he had just gotten out of the car with me. We both knew that nobody was going to be running out the back door of that house. This wasn't the home of a suspect–it was just a couple of kids that we had some questions for.

"She's going to grab the boys now. She asked to sit in on the questioning. I said sure–just hope it doesn't clam them boys up. And take it easy on 'em too, they're pretty bent out of shape about all of this."

"Let's hope not. There ain't nothin' at the scene, so we gotta get something out of those kids. Doubt there's anything on the body that will help us."

"So you'll go easy on the kids?" I asked again, this time with a bit more force behind my tone. Jack definitely needed reminding about something like that. He liked to rough people up.

"I'll do my best. You know me, I'm a big softie when it comes to the curtain climbers," he said with a shit eating grin.

He wasn't wrong, though. The crime scene didn't leave much for clues. Since the boys were the ones to find the body, hopefully they would have something useful to tell us. We stood and waited on the front porch for about five minutes while we waited.

The house had definitely seen better days. Paint was chipping off the walls around most of the exterior. The porch felt like it was going to cave in, especially at the landing after the top step, and someone had rigged a couple of the windows up with scotch tape, as the cracks spidered all the way up the sides. Maybe the neighborhood had changed for the better, but that house sure hadn't. We were only a little better than a decade removed from the Great Depression, and money was still tight in a lot of communities, this one included.

Returning with her sons, Mrs. Brown introduced them. "This is Clarence, Jr," she said of the taller of the two boys, "and this one here is John."

"Hiya, boys," I said in my most charming voice. "I'm Detective Denver, and this here is my partner, Detective Barnaby. We understand that you were the ones that found that lady this afternoon, is that correct?"

"Clarence found him," the younger one said, hiding half of his body behind his mother. "Tommy hit the ball over all of our heads, and Clarence ran to get it real fast so Tommy couldn't score. But when he didn't throw the ball back to us, we all went over to see where he was."

"Thank you, John," Jack said. "I bet that was pretty scary for you boys. We appreciate you taking the time to talk with us. Now, Clarence, what happened when you went to get your ball?"

"Um, the ball was laying right next to her foot. I stopped right there. I couldn't get any closer to it. I didn't know if one of the older kids was playing a prank on us or not, so I just stood there."

"I probably would've screamed and run away," I said. "You were very brave to stay there. What did you do next?"

"Like Johnny said, everyone else came over to see what I was staring at. We were all pretty freaked out by it. I ain't never seen a dead body before. Johnny ran back home and told Ma and she called the cops. After Johnny got back, we all were still staring at her."

"Did you see anybody else in the alley?" Jack asked.

"Not that I can think of. It was just us, I think," Clarence said, "but by then, I didn't know what to do, so I wasn't paying much attention to anybody else."

"Can you describe what you saw, exactly?" I asked him. "I know this was pretty scary for you, but everything you tell us will help us find the bad guy who did this to that poor woman."

"She was just laying there, not moving at all. There was blood on the ground around her. That's how I knew she was dead," he said, as he started sobbing.

"And was there anything else with her? A purse maybe? What about her shoes? Were they still on her feet?" Jack asked. We often did this back-and-forth procedure when questioning witnesses. That way we kept them off guard, and we were both able to watch for any tells when they responded to the other's questions.

"No, no purse or anything. Her shoes were both there, but only one was on her feet. The other was right next to our ball."

"Anything else that you can remember?" I asked.

"Tell 'em about the blanket, Clarence," John said as he came out from behind his mother's hips. A slight frown flashed across Mrs. Brown's face, but disappeared before I could decide what to make of it.

"What about a blanket, John?" Jack asked the younger boy. We both knew about the blanket already, but since neither of us had seen it yet, we didn't know what kind of shape it was in.

"Oh yeah, she was covered in a blanket so we couldn't see her face," Clarence added. "It smelled really bad, like somebody had taken it out of the trash and put it over her. It smelled like our garbage can does when Johnny forgets to take it back in the house after trash day."

"Okay, thank you, boys. If you remember anything else from today, have your mommy give us a call down at the station. You've both been a big help for us," I said, as I gave the three of them a smile. "You folks have a good rest of your Sunday and try not to let any of this get to you. We'll get the bad guy who did this, I promise you that."

Jack and I walked back to our car as the three of them went back inside their home. It was bad enough that this crime had happened in their neighborhood, but for those two young boys to be the ones that found her was an all out travesty. Those boys were too young to have to grow up that fast. The ills of the world shouldn't have reared its ugly heads to them at such a young age.

The whole thing was making me sick. This world was going to hell in a handbasket. I pulled out a flask from my pocket and took a huge gulp.

Jack looked at me, but didn't say anything. He never did. It was typical for me to take a few extra drinks here and there to help me get through my day–I just wasn't usually quite so brazen about it.

"Looks like we gotta head back to the alley and dive into that dumpster, Jackie Boy," I said, ignoring his stare.

"Looks like it." Jack finally looked away, shaking his head, but saying nothing. "Hopefully Davis and Miller are still there. We can get them to do the dirty work for us."

Chapter Three

B ack at the crime scene, I walked up to the dumpster and had a look inside.

It was pretty full. Not to the point of overflowing, but enough so that the lid wouldn't close. There was trash strewn all around it, too–typical of the city. I never could tell if people were just too lazy to walk the extra two feet to put their garbage inside of it, or if they were afraid of touching the filthy lid.

"Davis!" I shouted to the uniformed officer standing out on the sidewalk. "Give me a hand over here."

For some reason, Jack was still sitting in the car. I didn't have time to worry about that right now–we were going to run out of daylight soon. If we were going to get anything out of that dumpster, it would have to be right now.

"What gives, Max?" Officer Davis asked as he came over and stood next to me.

"Why don't you hop inside and start handing me some of the stuff off the top," I said, making it sound like more of an order than a suggestion.

"Why do I have to jump in? It's your case," he whined.

"Because your uniform is easier to wash than my suit is, you numb-skull. And because I said so. Now get in there. We're running out of daylight." As I helped him over the lip, I turned and shouted to his partner, "Miller, grab me some plastic bags out of the trunk of your car. We're gonna need something to put all of this shit in."

Davis started handing me things out of the dumpster. I stupidly hadn't grabbed any gloves out of our car, so I ended up soiling my suit after all. When Miller finally got there with the bags, I ordered him to start taking what Davis was handing over, and I went to see what was up with Jack, who was still sitting in the car.

"You okay, Jackie Boy?" I asked as I opened my side of the car and slipped in beside him.

"Yeah, I just needed a minute. Those two reminded me of mine when they were at that age, and it just hit me."

Jack had lost both of his sons, Denny, and Jack Jr., over the past 15 years. Jack Jr. got caught up in the rum running business, bootlegging booze for the Foggy Bottom Gang, back when prohibition was the law of the land. One night, he was picking up a supply in Virginia and got caught up in a trap at the state-line while he was trying to get back to the city. A chase ensued, and poor Jack Jr. hit a patch of black ice, lost control of his Coupe, and drove off of the Memorial Bridge. The car sank to the bottom of the river, and his body wasn't recovered for three whole days.

Jack never touched a drop of alcohol again after that. Even when some prankster at the precinct tried to spike his coffee one time, he spat it out and dumped the rest of the cup into the sink.

Now, Denny's was a completely different situation. Jack was extremely proud of his youngest boy. Denny was an airship rigger in the Navy. He enlisted right out of high school and was stationed in one of the territories out in the South Pacific. He, along with many of his brothers and sisters, never had a chance that fateful morning when the Japanese fighter pilots bombarded their base on Pearl Harbor. Denny perished in the attack, along with 2,403 other men and women. He was asleep in his bunk aboard the USS Arizona when the first bombs struck, just before 8:00 AM. He thought he was going to get the liberty to sleep in that day, unfortunately, he never woke up.

I had gotten pretty used to Jack's mood swings over the years, and most of the time I ignored them, or took an extra swig or two off of my flask to block out his occasional cold shoulder. But this time, I could see it was really getting to him.

"Well, let's get outta here then. Whaddaya say? Davis and Miller are going through the trash. If they find anything, they'll radio us. If not, it will be sitting on our desks when we get back to the station."

"What do you have in mind, Max?"

"How about the morgue?" I suggested.

The city morgue was in the Capitol Hill neighborhood of the city, which was only a few minutes' drive from where the crime scene was. "We gotta get there sometime tonight. Might as well head over there now."

"Sounds good to me. I'm no use to anybody if we're just going to sit here; I need to occupy my mind right now. Go tell them two yahoos that we're heading out."

"Deal," I said as I opened my door and got back out of the car.

They were none too pleased with my announcement, but that's the life of a uniformed copper. I could tell you stories for days about the shit I had to do back when I was in a uniform, or the scumbags I had to babysit while the suits were off doing god knows what. For now, my only job was to hop back in the car, and head off to the morgue.

On the way, I asked Jack, "You think it was symbolic how the blanket was placed over her body?" I knew Jack wouldn't want to talk about it while we drove, but it was eating at me.

"Whatcha mean?" He asked.

"You heard Clarence when he was telling us about the body. He said the blanket smelled like garbage. You think maybe we got some vigilante out here or something? Maybe the killer sees her as a piece of trash, so he does her right by the dumpster. Instead of throwing her in, he grabs the blanket out of the trash to throw on top of her--Like she's just a pile that didn't make it to its destination. Like maybe he thought she was lower than that. Maybe working dames was worse than trash in his eyes. Could even be one of them Bible thumpers that have been passing out those pamphlets all around town."

"Interesting. I honestly didn't even think of that. You may be onto something there, Maxey."

"I could be grasping at straws, but there was just something about the way the kid said it."

"When we get back to the station, let's have a word with Sarge about it. See if there's been anything else like this around town lately. Maybe he can put in a call to the other precincts and ask there, too. Can't hurt to go down this avenue. At least until we get other evidence. Right now we don't got nothin'."

The morgue was about a fifteen minute drive from the crime scene, so I clammed up to think more about my theory. Not just about the vigilante angle, but about those two boys as well. I couldn't get it out of my head how scared those boys looked. Knowing me, it was probably going to keep me up most of the night. Jack may do his thinking while he drives, but I do mine while I'm counting sheep.

"Denver, you copy?" A voice came over the radio. It was Davis, back at the crime scene.

"Roger that. Go ahead, Davis," I replied.

"We found a wallet in the trash. ID reads; Michael R. Morris. Address over in Georgetown."

"We just pulled up to the morgue. Bring it back to the station for us when you're done there. Along with everything else you pulled out of that scrap heap."

"Copy that."

As I looked over at Jack, his eyes told me that I'd heard the name over the radio correctly. Michael R. Morris wasn't just anybody. He was the mayor of Washington, D.C.

Chapter Four

"You think the mayor is behind this?" I asked Jack as we got out of our car and headed toward the front entrance of the city morgue.

"Dunno," Jack said as we walked, "but it *is* an election year, and he's been claiming he's going to clean up the filth in the city once and for all if he gets re-elected. But this seems too risky to me. Why would he do the dirty work himself? Don't make no sense to me one bit."

"Kinda what I was thinking too, but we're still gonna have to pay him a visit. You *do* realize that, dontcha, Jack?" I asked. He didn't say anything, but he definitely didn't look happy about it, either.

The Police Commissioner and the mayor were old college buddies. I think they went to Penn, or maybe Brown. Some yuckity-yuck Ivy League school that taught you how to be better than everyone else. Now I'm not saying that he's protected or anything, but we were going to have to tread carefully around the line of questioning that we would pursue. If the mayor felt threatened in any way from our presence, we would most definitely hear about it. Probably get thrown off the case to boot.

"Maybe we should pay him a visit at his house. Catch him off guard. It is Sunday after all," I continued.

"I like where your head's at, Maxey. That way, he can't hide behind his staff. It would be a bonus if his wife was there, too. Seeing him try to backpedal his way out of that in front of the old lady would be worth the price of admission."

"Damn straight," I said. "Nothing like making a house call on a weekend night."

"Nice of you two to finally show up, " a familiar female voice butted in, rudely interrupting us. "The body is being prepared for autopsy right now. Better get in there and have a look before it's too late."

The damn chalk fairy snuck up behind us while we were talking outside the front door. I wondered how much of our conversation she had heard.

"Sarah, nice to see you as always," I said, quickly plastering on a fake smile.

"Don't be a boob, Flattie. I know you're just glad I'm not gonna be in there with you. You ain't foolin' no one, Denver," she barked back.

"Feelin' a little frisky today, are we Toots? It's been a pleasure, as always." I smiled that same smile again for a brief second before adding, "Now get the hell outta my face."

"I wouldn't dare spend a second longer with your ugly mug even if they paid me," she shouted back as she rounded the corner and went out towards the lot.

"You sure yous two ain't gots the hots for each other, Maxey?" Jack asked with a laugh.

"Get bent, Jack," I said, giving him the evil eye. I flung the front door open with such force that I was afraid the window would break.

Okay, so maybe I was a little too harsh on him, especially since he seemed to finally be out of his little funk from back at the crime scene, but that broad got under my skin like nothing else, and Jack knew that.

Shaking my head, I went straight down the long hallway and in through the double doors that led into the lab. There wasn't much in the room except for a lone metal surgical table dead in the center above a floor drain, a sink in the corner, and a couple of rows of cabinets on the far wall. All I could see of the girl was her two feet that were sticking out the bottom of a white sheet that was placed over the length of her body. The tag that was tied to her toe was labeled "Jane Doe."

"Hey, Frank. Sarah said you were about to cut her open. Is that necessary for a gunshot vic?" I asked.

Frank Allcott was one of three medical examiners in the District. He worked nights and weekends, mostly. We ran into each other often enough to be on a first name basis.

"Max, what a surprise. Where's that grouchy old partner of yours?"

"I thought he was right behind me," I said, shrugging. "But who knows?" I nodded over towards Jane Doe. "So how's it look?"

"She took four to the chest. Looks like it was from pretty close range, from the bruising on her skin. You know, I heard one of the other MEs talking about these new tests that are supposed to be available soon. They call them ETIs. If I had access to that right now, I'd be able to tell you exactly where the shooter stood when he pulled the trigger. But until then, we'll just have to do things the hard way," he laughed. "But I can't tell which bullet was the kill shot as of yet, which is why I'm opening her up," he explained as he pulled the cover down and exposed her bare chest, showing me the damage.

The four entry wounds were in very close proximity to one another, which told me that either the shooter was really close, or he was a damn good shot. Have to make a mental note of that and check into the mayor's past to see if he has any firearms training.

Just as I was moving in to get a closer look at the wounds, I heard the doors open. I looked up to see Jack walking towards me with a scowl on his face. Frank filled him in on what he had just told me as I kept eying the bullet holes. I'm not a trained professional, and you see one bullet hole, you've seen them all, far as I'm concerned.

"How about down there?" I asked as I pointed to her pelvic region, wondering if this was a date that had turned sideways. "Look like there was any activity recently?"

"Hard to tell. I mean, by the looks of her, I would say she's a prostitute," Frank said, "but I can't see any tearing or bruising that makes it look like she was assaulted, if that's what you're asking."

"Just trying to piece this all together, Frank," I replied. "We got jack and shit from the crime scene. Oh, speaking of, where's the blanket that she rolled in here with?"

"I already sent that back to the station with one of your officers. I didn't get a good look at it, but I can tell you this much, that thing stunk to high heaven. I just wanted it out of my lab, to be honest," he said while holding his nose for effect. "She was found by a dumpster, right? Killer must've pulled it out of there and thrown it on top of her to hide her from the street view."

"That's what we're going on too. We've got Davis and Miller pulling trash out of the can to see if we can't come up with something," Jack said as he finally joined in. "All we know so far is that they recovered a wallet. But who's to say if that belonged to our guy or not?"

"Well gentlemen, if you've seen enough, I'd like to go ahead and find out which bullet killed her so I can get home and enjoy dinner with the wife for once," Frank said as he looked down at his watch. I hadn't even thought about the time, but it *was* nearing suppertime. If we were going to surprise the mayor with a visit, now would be the time to do it.

"I think we've seen all we need to see, Frank," I said as I looked towards Jack to see if he was going to interject. When he didn't say anything, I continued, "Keep us posted about what you find. My guess is the bullet at the top of her chest clipped one of her arteries and she bled out from the inside. But, hey, I don't want to do your job for you," I said with a chuckle.

"Alright, no need to show off, Max. You boys have yourself a good night, and I'll have a full report along with the size of the bullets on your desk before you get in tomorrow afternoon," he said, as we turned to leave the room. We said our thanks and headed back out the double doors.

"Listen, Maxey. About before," Jack started to say after we were back in the hallway walking towards the exit of the building.

"Don't worry about it, Jackie Boy," I interrupted, "Truth is, I'm the one should be apologizing to you. That broad gets under my skin, and I took it out on you. Truce?"

"Yeah, truce," he said as he stuck his hand out for me to shake.

That was a first. In all the years of us working together, through all of our little spats, this was the first time he'd ever stuck his hand out for a shake.

His clear mood swings made me think for a moment. He's on the verge of retirement. At least that's what he keeps telling me. If Nettie were still around, I bet that ship would've already sailed. Even though his mood swings were starting to get worse, as long as he stayed sharp, the PC wouldn't force his hand.

"Let's say we go pay that mayor of ours a visit," I said as I slammed the heavy steel car door shut behind me.

"Couldn't have suggested a better plan, Maxey."

Jack started the car and pulled out of the parking lot and onto Independence Avenue. I figured I should let the two stoolies over at the crime scene know our intentions.

"Davis, you copy?" I said over the car's radio as we headed off towards Georgetown, the swanky area of town that the mayor lived in.

"Davis here. What's your twenty?"

"We're off to pay our Mr. Morris a visit. But first I have a question for you boys."

"Shoot," Davis responded.

"Is that one of them dumpsters that has wheels on it, or is it flat on the ground?"

"Wheels. Why you ask, Maxey?"

"Get Miller to help you move it and see if you can't find any spent shells under it. After that, might as well rip down the tape and haul everything back to the station. Jack and I will be back shortly."

Chapter Five

The drive from Capitol Hill to Georgetown took about ten minutes if we stuck to Independence Avenue. There was probably a quicker route, but Jack was stuck in his ways. He only liked to take routes he was familiar with, and this was the route that he knew. I have to remind myself from time to time that when Jack came up through the ranks, the Metropolitan Police Department was still riding on horseback. Many of these roads didn't even exist when he was a rookie.

"Say, you know if the mayor was in the military?" I asked.

"Couldn't say. Don't know much about the guy other than him and the PC were buddies back in college. Why you ask?"

"Just that the shot groupings were real close together. Like the shooter knew how to handle a gat. Frank says he thinks it was done at close range, but even so, you don't know what you're doing and you're gonna be spraying lead all over the place."

"Very true. We'll have to do some digging on the down low after we get back to the station. Can't let anybody else catch wind of who we're looking into. That could be bad news for the both of us," he said as his face began to mess itself up again. Man, Jack really wore every emotion he had right there for everyone to see. I'd love to play poker with the guy, but his mood swings made being his partner challenging.

"So how you wanna play this when we get there?" I asked. We both knew the gravity of the situation we were about to embark on. One false move and the Commish could have both of our badges.

I normally didn't get nervous before we questioned a perp, but I could feel my blood pressure rising. I started to crave a drink, but I wasn't feeling brazen enough to take a swig right in front of Jack again.

"That's what I been trying to figure out," he replied. "Can't just barge in there and ask him where he was last night. That would put him on guard from the get go."

"What if we led with his lost wallet?" I suggested. "That way, it might seem like a friendly call."

"Good point. I'll let you handle it then," he said with a laugh.

"Of course you will, you bastard," I returned with a laugh of my own. "You wouldn't have it any other way, now would you?" In response, Jack just smiled. He knew he was a senior officer, and didn't have to do a damn thing he didn't want to.

The mayor lived in a three story white and gray manor that overlooked the Potomac River. The front porch was lined with pillars that made you think you were in some small town down south. It wasn't the nicest house, or the biggest, but it made me and Jack's places look like the slums in comparison.

Georgetown was old money. Slave money, to be exact. Lots of plantations and tobacco farming back in the day led to it being one of the most affluent neighborhoods in all of D.C. It was a fitting place for a politician to call home.

We pulled up and parked on the street, not wanting to make our presence known by pulling into the driveway. The mayor, of all people, would know our '47 Deluxe Tudor was department issued from a mile away. Even without the decals blazoned on the side and light bar over top, anybody in the know knew that ours was a copper's car.

We got out and walked up the long driveway. We climbed the two stairs up to the porch and I rapped my knuckles on the door, ignoring the gold door chime that was hanging on the wall right next to me. A minute went by with no answer, so I grabbed hold of the rope on the gold bell and gave the chime a few rings. I may have overdone it, as we heard the pattering of footsteps getting louder as someone urgently ran to answer it.

"Ello, what ees it?" A breathless woman asked in a south of the border accent. "I am trying to prepare the dinner for the Meester and the Meesus. They ask that you go now and maybe come back later."

I didn't doubt that they asked her to get rid of us, but unfortunately for her, we weren't going anywhere.

"I do apologize for the timing of this call, Senora," I said as I flashed my badge to her, "but if you could ask Mr. Morris if he would like to speak to us, we would really appreciate it. You see, we found his wallet, and wanted to offer him the chance to come retrieve it from the station with us. So, run along and see to it that you bring him back here, okay?"

Ten bucks says he was watching out the window from above and told his little house maid to get rid of us. That made me even more suspicious of the guy. And from the look on Jack's face, he was thinking the same thing I was. We would no doubt be hearing about this come Monday afternoon.

"Si, I mean, yes, Sir. I will go and get Meester Morris right now," she said, voice trembling.

Watching her run back towards the other room made me chuckle to myself. The power of the badge really tickles my fancy from time to time. I get a kick out of seeing the fear in a person's eyes when I flash my tin to them–especially when they're not expecting it. A few minutes passed before we heard footsteps approaching again, so I fished my badge and ID out of the inside pocket of my blazer, and waited for Morris to open the door.

"Officers," Morris said with a concerned look as he opened the door and had a look at us. "What could be so important that you had to disturb me during Sunday dinner with my family?"

"Hi there, Mr. Morris," I said, completely ignoring his question. "Did you happen to lose your wallet recently?"

"Actually, yes. Yes, I did." His body language went from defensive to thankful in the blink of an eye. "Did you find it?"

"We did," Jack said, taking the role of bad cop.

"Well, where is it? Can I have it back?" The mayor asked. His face was now showing concern. Man, it was fun to mess with people in authoritative positions.

"We actually don't have it with us," I said. "But if you'd like to take a ride down to the station with us, we could help you fill out the proper paperwork to get it back in your possession tonight. If not, it will probably be a little while before it could be released to you. You see, we're here as a courtesy, Mr. Mayor. We could probably get you your wallet back, no questions asked, if you took a little ride downtown with us."

"Why can't I just pick it up tomorrow on my way to the office?" He asked. The concerned face turned into one of fright. I still couldn't figure out whether or not he knew what was going on yet, though.

"Well, that's where things get a bit tricky on our side of things," Jack added. "Where did you lose it?"

"I honestly don't recall. If I did, it wouldn't be lost, now would it?" His defensive tone was sounding alarms in my brain. But he still hadn't said anything of use to us yet. Which was why I was about to drop the bombshell on him.

"No need to get testy. Like I said, we're here as a courtesy, Mr. Mayor," I said as I let him stew a bit longer. This was like foreplay to me. The ebb and flow of a questioning session is why I do the work. It's a powerful thing to be able to push and pull however you want, all the while the perp is lost like a deer in headlights, never knowing which of us to put their trust into.

"I suppose I could take a ride downtown with you, but I don't see what all the fuss is about over a lost wallet," he said, his fear apparent now.

"Grab your jacket. It's going to be a cold one tonight. Wouldn't want you catching cold when you have a city to run. We do all we can, but it's nothing without the mayor behind us, helping clean up the filth that is overflowing onto our streets. Ain't that right, Mr. Mayor?" Jack asked. He was toying with him at that point. The way he casually dropped in a line from one of Morris's campaign flyers was the icing on the cake.

"I don't think I like your tone, Officer," Morris replied. If he sounded defensive before, this was bordering on angry. He already knew something was up, but I don't think he knew exactly where we were going with this.

"Mr. Morris," I said, still trying my hand at playing the nice cop, "when do you last remember having your wallet on your person? Think about it long and hard."

"Yeah," Jack butted in, "it might look real bad for a fella in your position if your answer don't come back as truthful. So where was you when you lost your wallet?"

"I already told you, I don't remember. Kelly and I were down in Foggy Bottom for dinner out on the town. I had my wallet when we were there, as I paid for our meal. After that, we got in a cab and came straight back home. So I could've left it at the restaurant, or maybe it even fell out of my pocket in the car on the way back here. All I know is when I pulled the things out of my pants pockets when I was going to bed last night, my wallet wasn't there."

Sounded like an honest story to me, but I still had to press him a little more. "Did your car ride happen to pass through the FT?"

"No," he said matter-of-factly. "Why would it? That's the opposite direction from where we were going. As you can see, I live in George-town. The Federal Triangle is clear on the other side of town from where we were."

"Then you wanna tell me how your wallet ended up in a dumpster in a neighborhood right off the FT? And why it was lying right on top, directly above a dead broad that took four bullets to the chest sometime last night?" Jack asked, finally dropping the bomb that we had been dangling in front of the mayor's face for the past few minutes. I could see his face turning red from the blood that was boiling deep inside of him. Not that any of us like being lied to, but for Jack, it was something that he took overly personal.

"Oh my gosh, no. No!" He exclaimed. His eyes hit the floor, hands slightly shaking. He shuffled his feet, clearly unsure of himself and carefully considering his next move. Then, with an "ahem," he re-turned to his electable stoic persona, confidently returned my gaze, and responded calmly with, "I didn't have anything to do with any-thing like that. Ask Kelly. She'll tell you. We went out for dinner and we came right back here. Her and I sat in the reading room for the rest of the evening before turning in around 9:30. I swear, I had nothing to do with any dead girl."

That's what they all say, but the funny thing is, I believed him.

Chapter Six

We radioed a couple of sets of patrol officers to come in and take the statements of everyone at the Morris household while we drove back across town to the station, at a little after 8:00 PM. We left explicit instructions that each person was to be questioned separately and alone. By questioning each of them separately, it would be clear as day if one of them was lying.

As for Jack and I, we headed back to the station to comb through whatever trash Davis and Miller had dumped onto our desks.

"Jesus, what the hell is that smell?" I asked as we went through the front door of our precinct.

"I'm pretty sure that's what Davis and Miller dropped off for us," Jack said with a smirk.

"Lucky us," I returned.

When we turned the corner into the section of the station that our desks were in, I could see how the stench had reached the front door. There was a heap of trash about three feet high, right smack dab in the middle of my desk.

"Would you get a look at that, Maxey? This is why I try to play nice with the uniforms. Maybe you should give it a shot sometime," Jack laughed.

"Up yours, Jackie Boy, not like you're gettin' out of gettin' your hands dirty on this one," I returned with a laugh of my own.

We spent the next three hours going through bag after bag of trash without finding one single clue that looked like it could help us. I needed a little help to get through the thankless task, so I went to visit the bottle of Glenlivet I had stashed in my locker from time to time, blaming a "weak bladder" as I went.

"Hey, Jackie Boy," I said at around 11:30, "you haven't seen that wallet lying around anywhere, have you?"

"No, I haven't. I had forgotten about it, to be honest with you," he answered. "And same goes for that blanket too. That doesn't seem to be in this pile of trash either. Did Frank give you the name of the officer he gave it to?"

"No, just said he gave it to one of our guys. How much you wanna bet that wench Sarah took off with it?" I suggested.

From the look Jack gave me, it was pretty clear that he didn't think my attempt at being funny was appropriate.

"What is it with yous two, anyway?" He asked.

It wasn't something that I told anybody about, but Jack was right. We did have the hots for one another, or at least we did at one time. Not sure if the flame was still burning–especially after the one date we went on.

It was the first date I had attempted to go on after my old lady left me. I was still pretty messed up over things, and that was early in my heavy drinking days. I hadn't learned how to control it yet, not like I had now. I would drink a whole bottle in one sitting, not space it out over the course of eighteen hours, like I do these days.

We met at a crime scene. She was doing an outline of a body on a case that we had caught. I saw the way she was smiling at me, so I figured I'd give it a shot. Nothing worse than being lonely after your wife leaves you.

But it was different with her. I wanted to wine and dine Sarah, not just take her out for drinks at some dive. So I scored us some tickets to a show up on Black Broadway. Some really fancy joint in the 14th and U corridor called the Lincoln. We caught some cat named Cab Calloway that night. Sarah was into music more than I was, but I was happy just to be going out with a pretty girl on my arm.

It was all fine and dandy until the drinks started coming. I kept knocking 'em back and started to get a little too loud. Maybe I said a thing or two that I shouldn't have–I don't exactly remember. She got upset, slapped me across the face, called me a pig, and took off out of the building.

I didn't even try to go after her. My ego was bruised, and I was a little past three sheets to the wind. Needless to say, the date ended less than amicably, and we've never spoken about it since. It's been years now, and she doesn't seem like she's gotten over it either.

I shook my head, coming out of the memory. "It's none of your beeswax, Jack. Now drop it, or else." I said as I gave him a look.

"Or else, what, Max? What are you gonna do if I don't?" He asked, doubling down.

It had been a long day, and we had both been up and down too many times to count. Going from a sure thing, caught-red-handed perp, to a pile of junk sitting on our desks was putting us both over the top.

"Piss off, Jack. I'm going home. I'll see you tomorrow," I said as I grabbed my jacket and walked out of the precinct.

I walked briskly to Union Station to board the chariot that would take me back across the river towards my home. Maybe it was seeing Sarah, or maybe it was seeing that sweet young thing on the table with four bullet holes in her, or maybe it was seeing them two boys with tears in their eyes scared out of their wits. Whatever the reason, this case was already getting to me, and it hadn't even been twenty-four hours yet. The next few days were going to be rough—I could already feel that. Better make a mental note to bring my big flask with me tomorrow. I was definitely going to need it.

Chapter Seven

Once I was at home, I went straight for the liquor cabinet and poured myself a nightcap. My mind was spinning from the events of the day, and I was emotional and nostalgic. I usually had a drink to get to sleep, and today in particular I needed a little bit more of a kick than usual.

I kicked my feet back, looked up at the ceiling, and thought about how funny life could be. 10 years ago my wife met some rich guy from Shreveport who swept her off her feet. When she didn't show up for our court date, the judge awarded me the house. It's not much, but it's home. It's outside the city, and the long train ride home helps me decompress after work.

I couldn't stop thinking about the look that Jack gave me when I checked him for teasing me about Sarah. He didn't deserve that. It's not his fault I couldn't keep my emotions in check.

He once told me how he liked to curl up on his couch at night, light a fire, and read Agatha Christie novels before bed. I could actually see it, him drifting off to sleep with dreams that he was the real life Hercule Poirot floating through his head as he slept. But in reality, he read them because that was Nettie's favorite author. I guess it made his home feel less empty if he read something she enjoyed. I hoped I hadn't stopped him from enjoying the one thing he'd been looking forward to all day.

Before I went to bed, I set my alarm clock for an hour earlier than usual so I could have enough time to walk to the dime store on my way to the train station and pick him up a Christie classic. It was the least I could do for being such a jerk today.

We always did our best work when our two minds became one. Unfortunately, there had been very little of that out there today. Not at the crime scene, and definitely not at the morgue where we most needed it. I went to bed hoping that we would walk into the precinct the next day to some good news–that whoever took possession of the wallet was able to lift some prints off of the damn thing. That would go a long way towards mending things between me and Jack.

I tossed and turned, as usual, for about two hours before finally knocking off for the night. Must've been close to 4:00 AM. My neighborhood was so eerily quiet in the early morning hours that it made it hard to fall asleep at times–especially on the first night of a new case. Every time I closed my eyes I saw a flashback to them two boys, tears running down their faces, with the youngest one hiding behind their mother. Broke my heart, honest to god. Those two would never be able to unsee that sight for the rest of their lives.

Shit like that was what kept me up most nights. This world was becoming a mess. I guess that's what happens after wars break out. And we were still trying our best to recover after the big one, barely even five years ago.

I would say that's why I did the job, but that would be a lie. I do it for the paycheck–no more, no less. Not saying I ain't sympathetic to the ills of the world–it's just that I'm only one man. I couldn't possibly make a real difference.

That's probably why my outlook on life and the trash we have to deal with on a daily basis here in D.C. is as rosy as it is. That dame in the alley today was only the tip of the iceberg. There's a whole criminal underbelly in this city that we barely ever get a glimpse of. They're good–not like the people we run down for killing their wives, or the dope fiends we chase out of the parks at night. Those are the idiots–the easy ones to catch. Whatever difference I make is so insignificant that it doesn't even matter. There's just no help for this world anymore. Who knows–maybe that's the real reason I drink the way I do.

What I do know is that when my alarm goes off, I get up, shower, shave, and get back at it. That's all I can do–all anyone can do. It would be nice if I had a partner that I could count on–one who would have my back, no matter what. But I guess I'm the one to blame for that, in a way. I've got to try to make a change. If not for me, then at least for Jack. He doesn't have too many more years left, and he shouldn't have to work in fear that his partner might lose his cool at the drop of a dime.

When my alarm clock finally woke me up the next morning, I got up and poured myself a stiff drink. I felt that it was the only thing that would get me up and moving. The sky outside was gray, heavy clouds spitting rain. It didn't even have the decency to be a downpour–just a steady, disgusting drizzle that made everyone more depressed.

The phone rang just as I was about to hop in the shower. I wanted to ignore it, but thought better of it. Nobody rang me at my home unless it was important.

"Denver," I said as I picked up the receiver.

"Hey, Max, it's Jack."

"What gives, Jackie Boy? I'm about to hit the showers."

"Better try to get in as early as you can," he said. "We've got a new development in that dead bird case."

Chapter Eight

Muffled yells filled the air as the killer returned with an old, rusted-out linen cart.

"Two bodies will soon become only one..." murmured the killer, filling the warehouse with maniacal laughter.

Everything was going according to plan. Soon, the mayor would be framed, and they would be off, scott-free. Just a few more things to take care of.

Quietly, with a sinister smile on their face, they readied the second boody for deposit at the dump site.

I rushed back into the bathroom, splashed some cold water on my face, and threw on my clothes. I hoped the lieutenant was in a forgiving mood, because I didn't have time to shave. If I was so much as five minutes late for the metro, I would have to wait for the next train. And during lunchtime hours, that could mean an extra half hour wait.

The Monday through Friday lieutenant on our shift was a guy by the name of Ted McFweed. Some of the fellas called him "Teed McFweed" behind his back. A real ass kisser. He's the type of guy that wants to make PC by the time he's forty–and he probably will, too. As straight as they come, and he won't hesitate to take you down a notch for cutting corners. A real by-the-book type of cop.

McFweed was another one of those people that didn't see eye to eye with me. To put it bluntly, the two of us just didn't like each other. Neither of us was polite about it. I've tried nearly everything to get on his good side–even "killing him with kindness," which I don't do for anyone. Nothing's worked. Years ago, he pulled me out of an illegal gambling hall after I had had a bit too much to drink one night. I won't get into it now, but that was the beginning of the end for the two of us. He thinks a copper should be a copper twenty-four hours a day. Me? I think my personal time is my personal time. And there ain't nobody on this earth that can tell me differently.

I got to the station just in time to hop on the Yellow line that let off at Union Station. I couldn't help but wonder what kind of break we might have caught on the case. 'Ol Jackie Boy was pretty vague about it during his phone call. Maybe we got lucky and got some prints off of the wallet after all! Or maybe something on the blanket had pointed Jack in the right direction. Trying not to get my hopes up, I closed my eyes and tried to nap the rest of the way.

As I walked up the stone steps towards the front door of the precinct, I could see through the front window of the station that McFweed wasn't sitting at his desk–thank god for small miracles. Still, I opened the door as quietly as I could and slunk around the corner towards my desk.

Jack was already sitting at his. He held the receiver of his desk phone up to his ear in his left hand while he was jotting down some notes in his right. I gave him a nod as I plopped down into my own desk chair and started to look over the mess of paperwork that had gotten piled up over the course of the morning. The MEs report was on top, so I decided I might as well start there.

According to Frank, the slugs that he pulled out of the dead bird were .45 caliber. That didn't do much to narrow down the weapon of choice for our shooter, but it at least gave us something to go on. Most of the street thugs around these parts were pretty hot on the Colt 1911 these days. That gun fits the caliber of bullets that were used, so chances are, that would most likely be the type of gun we would be looking for. But that would be of no use to us unless we could find the man behind the gun.

"We got another body," Jack said as he hung up his phone. "Male vic, found in the same alley as the broad early this morning by a woman walking her dog."

"Jesus, you kidding me?" I said. That was not the news I was expecting to hear first thing today. "You think it's related?"

"If I were a betting man, I'd say one hundred percent."

"We get an ID on this one, at least?" I asked, still not really believing what I was hearing.

"Some hood who runs with the Penn Quarter Boys. Name's Webb, Kenneth Webb. Balthazar ID'd him on sight. Goes by the alias of Spida on the streets. He's small time, but was starting to make a name for himself around town. Had a couple of girls he was running out on the streets, turning tricks to pad his own wallet. Must've stepped on someone's toes, I'm guessing. Maybe that's why both him and the dame ended up dead." Jack explained.

I'm assuming Jack didn't get any sleep last night. Probably stayed here at the station and worked all the way through the night. He was prone to doing that from time to time–especially after Nettie had passed on.

"Spida, huh? What the hell kinda name is that?" I asked with a laugh.

"His name is Webb. As in Spida Webb," Jack said with a chuckle of his own. "It's not our job to understand the kids these days, Maxey. It's only our job to haul them in when they stray. And by the looks of things, somebody did that part of our job for us already."

"Sounds like it," I said as I shook my head in disbelief. "Anything on the blanket or the wallet yet?"

"Still haven't seen anything from the wallet. They're dusting it for prints on it now. If they find a match, they'll let us know, but, with how slow that process is, I wouldn't hold your breath," Jack said as he gave me that same look from the night before. I could tell he was still upset about things.

"Well, what's the plan, then?" I asked.

"Balthazar and Rooney are guarding the scene now. I assume Davis and Miller will be there shortly to spell them. The body is already back at the morgue, from what I hear, so we should probably go pay them a visit sometime soon. But first, let's go track down our dog walker and see what she's got to say."

"Sounds like a plan. Let me hit the head and I'll meet you at the car," I said, thinking this would be a great chance to grab a drink.

Walking down the hallway to the other side of the station, I took two long pulls off of the bottle and emptied the rest into my flask. A few sips ended up on the floor under my locker, but I let it be. Coppers are some of the biggest boozers on the planet. There's so much nastiness that we see on a daily basis that we have to learn how to cope with that one way or another. Some go home and take it out on their wives or kids. Others, their dogs. Me? I drink those ugly images away. And I'm not the only one, either. I bet if I opened every locker in this room, I'd find at least twelve bottles of booze. Even more if I went around desk to desk and started opening drawers. But I wouldn't want anybody airing my dirty laundry, so I keep it to myself.

When I walked outside, Jack was already behind the wheel of our car. As I got closer to the car, I could see he had a fat cigar in his mouth that he was chewing on. I've never seen him smoke one before, but from time to time he'll get to gnawing at one when he feels we're on the right track on a case.

"Where to first, then?" I asked. I wasn't sure if the lady with the dog lived in the same neighborhood as the alley or not, or if we even had an address for her yet, for that matter.

"Best stop by the crime scene to have a look around first. Then we'll go track down the dog walker. She lives on 14th and G. In some newer building with a few units in it. Shouldn't be too far from where the body was found."

"Good. We should walk the beat this time. Never know what we might come up with," I suggested.

Jack nodded, and then paused, obviously bothered by something. "You're still on my shit list, Denver. Don't push me over that edge today. That would not be a good idea."

I could tell he was serious. Jack didn't use curse words often, but when he did, I knew he was pissed. "Jack, listen," I tried to say, but he interrupted.

"No, *you* listen, Max. I've about had it with your selfishness. I've worked this job long enough to earn the respect of my partner. And if you can't appreciate that, then get the hell out of my life. I can get one of the younger guys who don't know squat to replace you. At least they obey orders and know how to respect their elders. I'm giving you one last chance, Maxey: Don't screw it up."

In all the years me and Jack had worked together, I had never heard an outburst like that from him. I felt like I'd been chided by a school principal, and I faced forward and was sure to keep my mouth shut. I peeked out of the corner of my eye to catch a look at Jack, but he was still fuming. The rest of this day was going to be miserable, I could already tell.

The crime scene looked all too familiar as we pulled up to it for the second day in a row. My hunch about the symbolism of the dumpster seemed to be coming true—no way this was just some random dump site, no pun intended. The chalk from yesterday's outline was still visible, as there was a new outline almost directly on top of it now.

Two bodies in twenty-four hours wasn't unheard of in this city, but two bodies on two separate days in the exact same place was. We were dealing with somebody who was trying to prove a point to us. We just had to find out who that somebody was, before more bodies started piling up.

Chapter Nine

We stood with the two other officers over the fresh outline in the alley. Officer Balthazar was explaining to Jack how he had collared Webb the week before for busting out the window of a storefront a couple of blocks north from where we stood. According to Webb, he was trying to get at a necklace that was displayed inside. He wanted to get something nice for one of his girls.

Just like it was yesterday, there wasn't much to see from the crime scene. And once again, there were no spent shells to collect. The alley looked a lot like it had the day before–except this time, the dumpster was empty. According to Balthazar, Webb had also been covered in a blanket right below the dumpster. I made a mental note to myself to try to recover both blankets before knocking off for the night. This was beginning to look like too much of a coincidence to not take a deeper look.

"You boys see how many bullets this guy took?" I asked, wondering if it was the same situation as we had yesterday.

"Yeah–four to the chest, from what we could see. Didn't get up close and personal with the guy, if that's what you're asking," he laughed. "But it looked like he had four holes in his shirt. I'm assuming that was from the gun-shot wounds," Balthazar explained to us.

"We'll have to take a look at the body over at the morgue, but this sounds like our guy. The dead bird from yesterday took four to the chest too," I told him.

"That's what we heard over the radio. These two must be connected somehow."

"From what I hear, he had a couple of dames he was running out here, so chances are, the broad from yesterday was one of his," Jack said in agreement. "I'm thinking this was probably someone else's turf, and they popped off a few in each of them to mark their territory—show them that this neighborhood isn't open for business."

"Makes sense," Balthazar replied. "These streets are turning into a war zone these days. I'm glad me and mine live across the river with the civilized folks."

"Ain't that the truth," I said with a sigh. "Well, Jackie Boy, wanna go hunt down that dog walker, then?"

"Yeah, let's get to it. You boys have a good rest of your day," he said to the two cops that were getting off shift. "Davis. Miller," he continued, "keep that radio close to you and radio us immediately if anything else comes up."

"I'll meet you up there, Jack," I said as I started off towards the street. "Something tells me that we're missing something here. I want some time to think—and who knows, maybe I'll stumble upon something along the way."

I left my mind to its own devices as I walked, crossing Pennsylvania on 12th instead of going over to 14th, lost in a mental fog. We now had two bodies. And since they were both found in the same location, I knew they were connected. One, a known thug, the other, a prostitute. *Could they be connected in a way that we're just not seeing yet?* It's the only conclusion that makes any sense. *But how, and why?* Questions like these are ones that normally showed their answer when you least expected them too. Hopefully, they would show themselves before another body did.

Nobody would be foolish enough to toss anything on a major thoroughfare, so I figured I'd have better luck on the side streets. G was only two streets up.

When I got to the intersection of 12th and G, I noticed a small pile of trash that seemed to have accumulated up against a lamppost outside of the little corner diner. The streets seemed to be pretty well kept up to this point, so it stuck out like a sore thumb. Monday morning was probably when the trash guys hit this part of town, I guessed.

I stuck the toe of my shoe into the mess to try to uncover the pile. Looked like a normal pile of trash that had gotten swept down the street by the winds before the rains brought it to its resting spot: A section of the morning paper, some wet leaves, a paper cup for coffee that was probably from the diner that I was standing outside of, and something that looked like it was made of a knitted material. Maybe a mitten or a stocking cap or something like that.

I didn't have any gloves or baggies with me, so I grabbed the wooden stirring stick out of the paper coffee cup and used that to move aside everything in the pile. As I shuffled the stuff around, the fabric became clear, and I could see that it wasn't a mitten or a cap at all. It looked to be the corner of a blanket that had been torn off. A gray patch that had some sort of black knitted pattern woven into it. Some sort of insignia, maybe? I couldn't tell, but it looked like it was one of a kind. If this was from one of the blankets used at the crime scenes, it would be easy to identify.

Excited, I jumped up, pulled out my badge and busted into the diner. Luckily, it was pretty empty. They were getting ready to shut down for the day, as most diners in town didn't stay open too long after the lunchtime hours were over.

"Detective Denver with the Metropolitan Police Department," I said as I held my badge up for everyone to see. "I'm on foot, and I don't have any evidence bags on me. I was wondering if you had a trash bag that I could use."

"Sure thing, hon," the lady behind the pastry shelf said. Her hair was tied up in a bun and she wore large horn-rimmed glasses, which seemed to be par for the course for her profession. "One sec," she said to me as she turned to her left, bent down, and pulled out a clear plastic bag from under the counter. "It sure is a shame to see more crime in our neighborhood."

"Yes, ma'am, it sure is," I said in my most thoughtful voice. "Thank you, ma'am. Yous folks have a good rest of your day."

Once back outside, I kicked myself for not grabbing a few more of them stir sticks while I was inside. Or even some napkins. I was so jazzed about finding that piece of blanket that my mind went scattered. I still had the stained and damp stirring stick that I was using before, so I used one foot to hold the bag in place, the other one to scoot the piece of fabric into it while I held the bag open with my left hand and tried to hold up the fabric with the stir stick in my right.

I'm sure it was a sight to see–thank god nobody was around. I probably looked like one of those drunks that you see wandering all over town.

With the fabric finally in the bag, I stood back up and hoofed it at a steady pace to meet up with Jack over by 14th and G.

Chapter Ten

J ust as I assumed, Jack was still sitting behind the wheel of our cruiser on the street outside the apartment house. He was staring out the window like he was lost in a deep daydream, and didn't even see me as I approached.

"Found something," I said as I knocked on the driver's side window and held up the plastic bag so he could see it.

"What the hell is that?" He asked grumpily, as if I actually had the gall to disturb him and knock him back into reality.

"It's a torn piece of a blanket," I answered, rather proud of myself, "don't know if it's from one of the blankets in question or not, but I figured it would be easier to grab it now then to try to find it again afterwards."

"Probably right," Jack said with a laugh while he shook his head. I bet he thought I wasn't going to find anything useful at all out there on my walk. "Now that you're here, let's go track down this lady so we can get to the morgue. I wanna be outta there before the evening traffic hits."

It didn't surprise me one bit that Jack hadn't even attempted to locate the dog walker yet. He was so stuck in his ways that it was starting to get to me. We were professionals, for Christ's sake. Our only goal right now was to solve this crime, not play the he-said-she-said bullshit games like we were back on the playground.

Stopping myself from lashing out, I took a deep breath. We had a criminal to catch, so I decided to take the high road. There would be other opportunities to deal with his bullshit later.

"Okay, Jackie Boy," I said with a dismayed chuckle, trying to not let my frustrations show, "point me in the right direction, and I'll go knock on the door. But you aren't going to sit back here and wait this time. Ain't nobody gonna be running out the back door of this place–ain't no back door to run out of."

"Fine," he said. "I'll be right behind you. She's in apartment 1B. Should be the second one down the pathway."

I waited until Jack was out of the car before I started on to the door. I've played this game before, and it's one I usually lose. Too many times I've been left looking like an idiot on the doorstep of someone's house, talking to myself, thinking that Jack is right behind me. We had been partners for well over a decade now, yet this was one thing I'd still fallen prey to far too many times to count. But not today. Not if he wanted us to bury the hatchet, at least.

"You gots a name for me, or am I just gonna go with ma'am?" I asked as he saw I wasn't taking another step until he was right there next to me on the sidewalk.

"Anglin," he said. "I believe her first name is Marie, but I might've misheard that. Best to stick with Miss Anglin."

"Sure thing, Jackie Boy," I said as I started towards her front door.

The building looked to be one of the newer ones in town. The paint was still as white as could be. Couldn't say the same thing for any of the other buildings on the block. Over the past decade, new tenements were starting to pop up left and right all throughout the city. Not that this was a bad thing, but it sure wasn't helping with the crime rate. A new building like this probably brought in higher income folks to the neighborhood, but when you still had the slums only a few minutes away, it seemed like it was counterproductive to me. Now there was just nicer stuff in the neighborhood for these lowlifes to steal. But, like I said before, change doesn't happen overnight. You have to start somewhere. My guess is that this will probably be an extremely nice part of town come twenty to thirty years from now. But today, it was just a shiny new building in the middle of a trashy neighborhood. You know what they say about tying a ribbon on a pile of shit, and all.

I looked back to make sure Jack was still with me as I knocked on the door. There was no immediate answer, but we did hear yapping from a dog on the other side of the door. The thing with buildings like this was, it was damn near impossible to tell if someone was at home or not. Not like when you pull up to a house. There, you can see if there's a car in the driveway, but not in a building that houses several people. There were five cars in the lot, not counting ours.

I knocked again, but there was still no answer. By this time, I was ready to give up and head over to the morgue, but Jack shouldered his way past me and gave the door a good thumping. The dog inside seemed to go ballistic from all the pounding we were doing. There was no way there was a person in there, not with the carrying on that that dog was producing.

I fished a card with our names and the station's phone number on it out of my jacket pocket and stuffed it inside the door jamb. Jack shrugged his shoulders at me and turned to head back towards the car. I took one last look back at the front door as I was heading back to the car and noticed that the card I had placed in the jamb, not even five seconds before, was missing.

Maybe this lady didn't feel like reliving the horrors she had witnessed earlier that morning. I couldn't fault her for that. But the easiest way to show up on a copper's shit list is to not answer the door when they come 'a knocking. Miss Marie Anglin, or whatever her name is, would definitely be on my radar now.

Chapter Eleven

W e took 14th down to Independence and hung a left, on our way to see a body in the morgue for the second day in a row. Jack and I both stared out the front window, lost in thought. My mind kept going back to those two blankets. It still didn't make any sense to me how we hadn't been able to take a look at them yet–like there was some sort of conspiracy floating around them damn things, and everybody was in on it to keep them away from me and Jack. I pulled the plastic bag with the piece of fabric in it out of my pocket and examined it for a few seconds before picking up the handheld radio off of our dash so I could call in to the station.

"McFweed, you copy?" I asked

"McFweed, here, go ahead," the voice on the other end of the radio said to me.

"Denver, with Barnaby, here. I found a piece of blanket near the crime scenes over in the FT today. Me and Jack still haven't had a chance to look over either of the blankets that were recovered yet. Was wondering if you could give a description to us. We're on our way to the morgue now to get a look at the second vic," I said, trying to keep it as professional as I possibly could. I didn't need, or want, to be putting out two fires today.

"Copy that. They're both still in evidence. I ain't even seen 'em yet, myself."

"Roger that, Ted," I said, thinking the conversation was over. But the next thing I heard knocked me for a loop.

"Actually, we got an anonymous tip a few minutes ago," the lieutenant continued. "Seems like a hooded figure with a limp was spotted in and around the alley the past two nights. The caller couldn't make out if it was a man or a woman, but they thought there was something that looked like the butt end of a gun sticking out of his or her jacket pocket. So be on the lookout for a person matching that description in the area."

"Will do. They think it's one of the thugs from the 'hood, then?" I asked.

"No, they think it was someone a bit older than they're used to causing problems in the area. But it wouldn't hurt to check out the Penn Quarter Boys. Maybe keep an eye on them tonight."

"Copy that. We'll get Davis and Miller to stake 'em out after they leave the crime scene."

"Maybe yous two should stakeout the area around the alley tonight, too. Couldn't hurt, not with two dead bodies left there on two consecutive nights."

I groaned at that idea immediately, but I knew the lieutenant was right. This might be the first break we've had in this case so far. "Roger that. We'll be on the radio if needed."

"Copy that. Thanks, boys. McFweed out," the lieutenant said as I heard him click off.

Great, I thought to myself as I patted my inside jacket pocket, trying to gauge how much hooch I had left. I hadn't had a pull since we left the station. But if I was going to be trapped in this car all night long with Jack, I was going to have to get creative about things. No way

I could pull an all-nighter as sober as a nun, that was for damn sure. That also meant I was going to have to find a way to get a refill, too–I didn't have enough on me to last a whole extra shift.

"Hey, Maxey," Jack said after I placed the radio back in its holster. His voice was trembling in fear as he looked to be on the verge of tears, "I gots something I need to get off my chest."

"Sure, Jackie Boy. What is it?" I asked, as concern crept over my whole body.

"Well, I've been trying to find a way to sugarcoat this for you all day, but since there's no easy way around it, here goes: I was in early this morning because I had my annual check-up with the company Doc." he said, as tears started to roll out of his eyelids, down his chin, and onto his blazer and shirt front. He started to speak again, but was overcome with a fit of tears as his shaky voice gave way to blubbering nonsense that I couldn't understand. Finally, after that wave of emotion subsided, he confided in me: "It's not good, Maxey,"

"Truth is, I'm not gonna be around much longer. I had to beg the PC just to let me finish out this case." He paused, as if his mouth couldn't form the words that his mind was trying to convey. His focus shifted from my face to a bird that flew by overhead. The smile that crept up, although brief, proved how dire the situation truly was.

"My brain ain't what it used to be, from what them tests say. My reflexes are shot, my vision stinks, even with my glasses, and my hearing just ain't what it used to be either. Basically, they want to send me out to pasture."

I felt for the guy. This wasn't how this was supposed to go down. Jack was a living legend in the MPD. He should be going out on his terms, and with a hero's salute. A ceremony for fifty years of service, even–any other way than this. This didn't seem right to me.

"I got the okay from the PC to finish this case, but if we don't haul in a suspect fast, I think I'm gonna get the boot. They already have a new partner lined up for you for when I go–that young up and comer, Cole Diamond–but I just wanted you to know that I love you like a son, Maxey. You've given me comfort when I thought all else was lost. And I thank you from the bottom of my heart for that." He pulled over, unable to choke back tears.

I was taken aback by the news he had just told me. My body went numb. At least now I knew what was going on with him, but that did little to help the situation. Plus, it made me feel lower than low for getting mad at the guy. I knew I should say something, but I didn't know what. We sat without speaking for a good ten minutes. The only sound in the car at all was the whimpering of an old, beat up and broken man. I, too, fought back tears as I wondered how I would get on without my mentor in this job. I knew of Cole Diamond, but I didn't know him personally. And the idea of working with someone else scared me to death. Especially if I was going to be the elder officer that the young kid looked up to.

I looked over at Jack to see if the tears had stopped yet, and he turned and looked back at me with a look that tore right into my heartstrings.

"Maxey?" He asked. His voice was still trembling something fierce.

"Yeah, Jackie Boy?" I asked in return.

With dampened eyes, he said, "Let's go bag us a bad guy. Whaddya say?" His demeanor changed instantaneously, letting me know that, at least for now, he was back in the game.

Chapter Twelve

As we pulled back out onto the street, I noticed a smile creep up on Jack's lips. Maybe getting that news off of his chest had done some good for him. It seemed to do some good for me, that's for damn sure. Gone was the animosity that I had been feeling ever since last night, and in its place was a newfound feeling of pride and vigor. That lit a fire under me like nothing else had in months. If this was going to be his last case, we were going to find this scumbag and bring him to justice tonight. That was all there was to it.

We sure had our work cut out for us, though, and that was putting it mildly. All we had to go on was the description of a hooded figure that walked with a limp—we didn't even know if it was a broad or a bundie that we were looking for yet. Could be tied to the Penn Quarter Boys, could be tied to the mayor, for all we knew. And we'd only interviewed two sets of folks so far, with nothing coming from either one of them. We just didn't have much to go off of. And those damn blankets seemed to be holding more cards than a swindler at a Saturday evening Hold 'Em game. The odds were not in our favor.

When we pulled up to the morgue, it felt like déjà vu. The old stone building had the same dreary look to it as it did the day before, but the clouds, rain, and gray skies that hovered above the building gave it a more menacing look to it today under that evil-looking sky.

"Well, well, well," Frank said to us as we walked in, "look what the cat dragged in. You know, I've got this funny feeling I can't shake that I've seen yous two before recently."

We all three laughed at that.

"Where's Madison? Ain't he normally here Mondays?" Jack asked out of curiosity.

"He had some time off coming. Think he went down south to get some sun in before the long winter hits. Don't blame him. I'd do the same thing if I could afford it. Hell, if they offered me a job in Miami, I'd agitate that gravel without thinking twice," Frank explained.

"Me and Nettie thought about it once," Jack added, "then the Depression hit, and you know the rest. Maybe in retirement, but I don't wanna think about that right now."

"You're as spry today as the day I first met you, Barnaby. I don't think you'll have to worry about that for quite a while," Frank responded with a warm smile. There was no way he could have had a clue about what the two of us had just talked about in the car ride over here.

"So, Frank," I asked, quickly trying to get off the subject of retirement before Jack got his face all messed up with emotions again, "What's it look like on this one? Same as before?"

"It's almost identical, Maxey," he said with a shake of his head and a puzzled look on his face. "If you took an outline of the bullet groupings from yesterday and laid them on top of the vic here, it would nearly match up completely."

"Ain't that something," Jack added. I could see a mist of dampness starting to well up in his eyes. Best to keep this conversation on the dead body, if I could.

"It really is," Frank continued. "Whoever shot these two people definitely knows how to handle a weapon."

"Sure sounds like it. Anything stick out at you on this one specifically?" I asked.

"Not really. It looks like it's on the stick, if you ask me. Still, I'm gonna open him up and take a look inside. I'm willing to bet I'll find the same caliber of slugs as I did yesterday. There's no way two different people did this. Not with how similar the shooting pattern is."

"Okay thanks, Frank. If you ain't gots anything to razz our berries, we'd best to get back at it. We gots us a fresh tip, and there's gonna be a lotta moving parts to get situated before nightfall," Jack said, taking over his role of the alpha voice once again.

"Nope, think this one reads like a book. I think I can handle this on my own from here on out. I'll get you the report as soon as I'm done with it. The wife was happy after I made it home in time for dinner last night, so I'm in no rush to get home today. Probably drop it off to yous before the end of your shift."

"Thanks, Frank. We'd appreciate that," I said as we shook hands and headed back out the door.

I never truly liked being in the morgue, but after what 'Ol Jackie Boy had told me about his health earlier, this place seemed to have a new aura of despair hovering over it. It was almost like I envisioned myself having to come down here in the middle of the night to ID Jack or something. I excused myself to the restroom and took a swig. I think this might be tougher on me than I originally thought. Jack was more than just my partner–he was family.

After I hit the head, I took one more pull off of my flask and headed back out to the car. We were just getting started, and I knew the night was gonna be a long one.

"Before the thought even crosses your mind, Maxey, I ain't knocking off early," Jack said with a stern look on his face as I climbed into the car.

"I wouldn't even think it, Jackie Boy," I said back, "We got one shot at this. I ain't letting nobody send you out to pasture until you're damn well ready to do it yourself. We close this tonight, you ain't gotta be worried about a thing. I guarantee it."

"Damn straight, Maxey. PC wants me out, he's gonna have to drag me off the job kicking and screaming. I ain't never rolled over on no one, and I ain't gonna make you the first victim. I finish what I start. And that's the gods' honest truth. Let's get back to the station and get our hands on those damn blankets before we have to get back out on the streets."

"Amen to that, Jackie Boy," I said to him in a reassuring tone, "The sooner we get this perp caught, the better."

Chapter Thirteen

C ole Diamond was getting briefed on the situation as we walked back in through the front door of the station. He shot me a look as McFweed was talking to him, which I couldn't quite get a read on. Diamond wasn't exactly a rook, but he was fresh to plain clothes. He was as wet behind the ears as a baby at a baptism. Hopefully I won't have to worry about that challenge just yet. Nope, I'd have at least the rest of the night before I'd have that handful on my plate.

"McFweed," I said as I walked by the two of them. "I'd like a word when the two of yous are finished, please."

He blew me off and continued speaking directly to Diamond. I sighed and took a seat at my desk while Jack went to go roundup the blankets and get an update on the prints that they had pulled off of the wallet.

Looking across at Jack's desk, the gravity of the situation hit me. I snuck a quick pull off of my flask and wiped the tears out of my eyes with the back of my paw. Yeah, I had to admit it–this was going to be rough on me.

As I changed my view from Jack's desk to my own, I noticed something new there. A pink memo note placed on top of everything else, notifying me that a Miss Anglin called while we were out. Luckily enough for us, whoever took the note also got the phone number. I picked up my desk phone and dialed just as Jack approached our desk area with a folded piece of paper in one hand and two plastic bags in the other. Excited to see the evidence, I decided to hang up before she had a chance to answer. I could deal with Miss Anglin later.

"Whatcha got?" I asked as he placed the items in front of me on my desk.

"Two blankets, and a positive ID on them prints they lifted off the wallet. You're never gonna believe who the prints belong to, either."

"Who?" I asked with a puzzled look on my face.

"Take a look for yourself, Maxey. It's all right there in front of you."

I opened up the folded piece of paper and my jaw dropped at the sight of the name I read in bold print on the top of the page: Kenneth Webb. Our dead vic from this morning.

"Can't be a coincidence, you think?" I asked, looking at Jack's similarly amazed reaction.

"I wouldn't count on it. I'm gonna see if McFweed can't put a call in to the PC. Ask him how he wants to handle this. Not like we can go and drag the mayor in here ourselves. Too many folks would see that. This is gonna have to be dealt with in a very delicate manner. Otherwise, we'll have press from all three of the stations here faster than bees on an open jar of honey."

"Probably right, Jackie Boy," I replied. "While you're doing that, I'm gonna open up these blankets and see what I can find." As Jack took his leave to the lieutenant's desk, I opened up the two evidence bags in front of me, pulling out the plastic bag holding the scrap out of my pocket as well.

Once all three items were laid out on my desk, it was pretty clear that they were one and the same. The scrap I found on the street today looked to be the corner of the half of the blanket that was used to cover the dead bird. I matched it up next to the larger piece. It was an exact fit—even the frayed edges of both pieces matched up perfectly. It didn't look to be as clean as the cut that went through the middle of the blanket when I matched up the two larger pieces. That cut was precise. Probably from a pair of linen sheers, I was thinking. The corner piece looked more like it was torn. Like it was an accident.

Still, it didn't tell us anything except that the killer had at least planned on using the blanket before they did the deed. It didn't get us any closer to figuring out who this mystery person was. We had the prints of the dead guy from today on the wallet we found next to the dead broad yesterday. This at least pointed us towards a clear cut suspect: Michael Morris. Mayor of D.C.

I still had my doubts about the mayor actually pulling this off himself—he probably had people to do his dirty work for him. Now I know that politicians are known to be smooth talkers—in fact, most are trained on the subject. But the sincerity in his voice and in his eyes last night seemed to be as legitimate as they come. But like I said, they're trained to lie to the public. Plus, if he had one of his people do the killings, it would be easier for him to lie to our faces. And if that were the case, it would be a hell of a lot harder to pin this on him, too.

But we needed to make him sweat. We wouldn't be doing our job to the fullest if we didn't haul him in for a second round of questioning. Put him at the table in the interview room and turn up the heat on him to see how he fared against me and Jack's rapid fire questioning coming at him from all directions. That's how you break a perp—you've got to be the one controlling the environment.

I only hoped that we weren't risking our jobs here. The mayor was still a close friend of the Commissioner. So we had better be one hundred percent right about him being our guy. This wouldn't be the first time I've been wrong on a hunch, but I've never feared for my job before like the way I did right now.

Bringing the mayor in and sitting him down in the interrogation room would be the only way to tell if he was being truthful with us or not. We had broken many a suspect in that tiny room. That table had seen more confessional tears than a hankie at a funeral. That was our war room, where Jack and I flourished the most. If the mayor was behind the shootings, we would get to the bottom of it within an hour.

This wouldn't be the first time we would be face to face with a politician. This is Washington D.C. after all, and politicians were in every corner in the city. Most of them were as crooked as the crooks.

But I've got to stop thinking of this perp as the mayor. He still holds the upper hand that way. No, he's just another creep that we're going to be questioning. He's Michael Morris. An average citizen who's been put in our crosshairs. A suspect who looks to be the person who gunned down two people. No more, no less.

Chapter Fourteen

It was a waiting game now. My least favorite part of the job. Especially since we didn't have the go ahead to nab the perp ourselves. As I looked at my watch, I saw it was just about dinner time—which would be the perfect time to catch the mayor off guard for the second night in a row.

I looked up from the blankets for a moment to see Jack returning from the other room. For once, I couldn't get a read from his face as to how his conversation with McFweed had gone.

"McFweed just got off the horn with the Commish," Jack said as he took a seat at his desk. "He's taking Diamond with him to get the mayor and his wife right now. My guess is we'll get a shot at Morris while they take the wife in another room. I don't know about you, but I'd like a shot at her, too. Especially since we didn't get a chance to talk to her last night."

"I'm right there with ya, Jackie Boy. They may have had a chance to collaborate their stories after our surprise visit last night, but she don't stand a chance against us in that box."

"Nope, and we have them dead to rights with the prints off of his wallet," Jack said as he seemed to get excited about all of this all of a sudden. "He's gonna be on a plane destined for Alcatraz before he even knows what hit him."

He must've been feeling better about things after all. That tends to happen when we catch a break in a case, especially one of this magnitude. The mayor was a name that everyone in town would know, and our names would be right next to his in the papers. So we needed to go about things this time around in more of a classy manner—one that would keep it civil in the press.

"I don't mean to rattle your cage or nothing, Jackie Boy, but we ain't even talked to him yet," I said, " Let's just see how it plays out.?"

"You're right, Maxey. I guess I just got caught up in the moment. The PC is gonna be all over me as it is, and not just for having McFweed make that call, either. I'm gonna be under a magnifying glass for the rest of my time behind the badge. I just wanna nail this guy tonight."

"I know you do, Jack, and I do too," I said in my most reassuring voice, "but we gotta take step one first before we can take another. Sound familiar? You taught me that nearly twenty years ago. We can't get ahead of ourselves."

"I know, I know," he said as he let out a big sigh and stared down at the ground under his desk. "This waiting is killing me. I wish it was us that went and got that bastard and his wife. At least then we could get a read on them in the car. We're gonna be going into that room cold. Them two will hold all the momentum, not us."

"Maybe. But maybe not though, too. The smug bastard probably thought he got rid of us once and for all last night. There's no way they was expecting for another car to show up at their house tonight to drag them in for questioning. They'll be knocked off guard by that, and that's when we pounce on them like a lion on a hare. We hold the evidence, Jackie Boy, not them. We still hold the upper hand. Okay?"

I felt like the tables had turned all of a sudden and I was the mentor while Jack was the student. He was probably so mentally exhausted that he didn't even realize it. I'm normally the hot head who has to be held back, not Jack. He's normally calm and collected under the stress of the job. I'm the one sneaking off, taking drinks to calm my nerves down several times a day while he holds everything together. This was uncharted territory for me.

As I looked around the room, I realized that me and Jack were the only two left at our desks. All the noise had disappeared from the room as I was trying to get the situation under control. It was eerily quiet in a room that was normally filled with all sorts of different noises, and it made me wonder if something else was going on.

The moment that thought passed through my brain, I saw the reason for the lack of noise as Russell Blades, the Police Commissioner, rounded the corner and headed straight for our two desks.

"Denver, Barnaby, listen up," the Commissioner barked at us. "I'm taking the lead on the questioning. You two can watch from the other side of the window if you want, but Mike is a friend of mine—not to mention my boss. This needs a delicate touch, and frankly, I don't think the two of you have it. I don't want to hear any complaints about it from either of you. My word is final. Understand?"

"I understand, Sir," I said, mad as hell at losing the chance to question the perp, but trying to stay professional. "But if Jack and I can't get in there for questioning, why on earth were we assigned the case?"

"I don't think I like where this is headed, Denver," he snarled back at me. "This is still your case, but I don't think you two have what it takes to question a perp of this stature. No more, no less. Besides, last I checked, I was your boss. Make more sense to you now?"

"Yes, Sir. We understand." Jack butted in, though I doubt he knew what I was going to ask.

"Sir," I continued before Jack could add anymore, "you know the mayor well. Do you know if he owns a firearm, or if he has any formal firearms training? The groupings on both victims were very precise.

An untrained shooter would not be able to pull that off on two separate victims on a whim."

"Don't forget who you're talking to, Denver. I was once in your position. I'm a copper, same as you. I wear my tin with as much appreciation and gratitude as the next guy. You don't end up commissioner out of luck, Max. I earned this title through years and years of hard work making my way up through the ranks. That is why I, and not you two, will be leading the questioning. Until he's placed under arrest, he is still the acting leader of this city, and he deserves to be treated with respect. As for your question–don't worry, I've seen the reports. I'm well aware of all the details held within them. I'm sure I'll ask all the questions you've thought of, and then some. "

"Well, Maxey," Jack said to me after the commissioner was out of earshot, "What's say we go take our seats for the show. Don't want to miss anything."

"Might as well. Ain't gonna get to the bottom of this sitting here and sulking." I responded as I got up off of my chair and led the two of us to the small closet sized room adjacent to the interview room. There was a window in there where we could watch what was happening during the questioning. The microphone that was fixed to the center of the table led to a speaker on the other side of the two-way mirror, so we would be able to hear everything the PC asked as well. The only problem was, we could only be in one place at one time, so if they were questioning the wife in another room, we'd be out of luck.

The minutes ticked by slowly as we awaited the entrance of the mayor and the commissioner. I checked my watch every few seconds, hoping that the next time I looked up it would be show time. But the minutes kept ticking on by. I was about to excuse myself to go sneak a drink when I finally heard the door open on the other side of the wall.

McFweed led the mayor in and sat him down at the table as Diamond joined us in the tiny room on the other side of the wall. Since the mayor came in on his own, there was no need to shackle him to the hook at the center of the table. McFweed took a seat across from him and placed a file folder on the table in front of him. There was still no sign of the commissioner yet.

"What gives, guys?" Diamond asked as he looked at the both of us to see our expressions. We both could tell this was the first time he'd been holed up on the other side of an interrogation.

"Beats me," Jack answered, "but he ain't said nothing yet. Maybe the PC needed to hit the head first or something."

In all actuality, the commissioner was making his friend sweat. He was balking at entering the room while McFweed leafed through the files on the table, deliberately making sure that the mayor got a good look at the photos of the bloody victims and the crime scene at the same time.

It was a ploy that me and Jack had used from time to time. We saved it for the perps who thought they were smug enough to fool us, and at this point in time, I think the mayor definitely fell into that category. After a few minutes of that charade, the commissioner finally entered the room and took his seat next to McFweed.

"Hi, Mike," the PC said, "quite a situation we find ourselves in, isn't it?"

Chapter Fifteen

As those three men sat at the table in the interview room, the three of us stood in the room next door, listening in and watching the mayor of our city start to squirm from the opening salvo delivered by the PC.

"What the hell is going on, Russ?" Morris asked. "First your guys interrupted my dinner last night, and now they've gone and drug me in here tonight. And for what? You know me, Russ, I didn't do this."

"I do know you, Mike," the PC interjected sternly, "and that's why it's me in here asking the questions, and not two of my detectives. They wouldn't give two shits about who you are. But I do, so let's get to the bottom of this, okay?"

"Okay, but I don't know what to tell you that I already didn't tell the whole slew of officers you sent my way yesterday. Whatcha want to know, then?"

"For starters, do you keep a gun in the house?"

"No, you know that already, Russ. You know that as an elected official, I thought it would be best if I didn't hold any weapons in or around me or my property. I don't have any at my home, and I sure as hell don't have any at my office downtown, either."

"We've got people searching your house as we speak, so you had better hope they don't come up with anything," the commissioner said, giving his friend across the table from him a look. "It definitely would not look favorably for you if you were found to be lying to me right now."

"Jesus, Russ. You have people going through the house? I have collectibles in there. You've seen them! Old guns from the Civil War. If those get ruined, you'd better bet your ass there will be hell to pay. Besides, they're all pinned. They don't even shoot ammo anymore. They're just wall decorations," the mayor pleaded, "You know this. You've held them in your hands before."

"I do know this, but for that reason, it raises suspicion about you. Being an avid gun collector and all. Now tell me, where did you lose your wallet again? That seems to be where all of this started."

"Like I told your officers yesterday, I have got no clue where I lost it. If I did, it wouldn't be lost."

As questioning continued, the mayor was slowly falling apart. His hair was disheveled, and his hands went from being clenched in front of him on the table to holding his head, clenched in fear. I still couldn't get a great read on the guy, but if you asked me right then, I'd say he was behaving in the manner of a man who didn't understand why he was being questioned.

"Then humor me, Mike. Where's the last place you remember having your wallet?" The PC asked as he eased up the tone of his voice slightly.

"Once again, like I told your guys yesterday, the last time I held my wallet in my hands was at the restaurant when I paid for our meal. I didn't realize it was missing until we were already home and I was taking things out of my pockets before going to bed."

So far, the story was adding up from what he told us yesterday. Pretty much damn near verbatim, actually. Sometimes that's a good thing, meaning the perp is being honest with us, but other times it's not. Like the words were from a script that was learned from a person knowing they were going to be questioned. It was far too early in the interrogation to make that assumption just yet. But to have the same story two days in a row told me quite a lot. For starters, we may have an innocent man on our hands.

"And you and Kelly took a cab on the way home, is that correct?" McFweed asked, as he finally saw an opening into the action.

"Yes, that is correct. God, don't your guys share any of this information with their superiors? This is all what I went over last night with them."

"How did you pay for the cab without your wallet?" McFweed continued.

"Kelly paid the cab driver with a couple of bills that she had in her purse. That's how we've always done it. If I'm buying the meal, she pays for the cab fare. It's been that way ever since we first started dating. She always felt that it wasn't fair for the burden to fall on me if we wanted to go out on a date."

McFweed and the commissioner seemed to not even hear that answer, as if it didn't line up with their narrative. But for me, it backed up my assumption that he really did lose his wallet. So much for the PC taking it easy on his friend.

"Who is Kenneth Webb to you, Mike?" the PC continued, as he jumped back in with that question from way out in left field. "Where's he fit into all of this?"

"I don't know any Kenneth Webb. I've got no idea what you're talking about."

"I see," the commissioner said as he looked down at the picture of Webb, gunned down in the alley. "So, this person here means nothing to you?" He asked as he flipped the picture and put it right in front of Morris.

The mayor said nothing as he started weeping, looking at the photo through his fingers as he covered his face in increasing horror.

"What about this one?" The commissioner continued as he slung the picture of the dead broad towards Morris as well. "You know her, Mike? She one of your girlfriends that didn't take the hint when you tried to break it off? Huh? Were you afraid Kelly was gonna find out about your extramarital affairs and kick you to the curb? Is that what happened? You devised this whole story of the stolen wallet just so you could keep your dirty little secret safe?"

Throwing the pictures at the mayor, the PC crossed his arms in contempt and leaned back in his chair as though he'd won. "You disgust me, Morris."

"No, no, no," the mayor replied. "I've never seen either of these people before in my life. You have to believe me, Russ. I do not know what is happening here. Am I being set up? I took my wife out for a night on the town, and now you're giving me the third degree about killing two people?"

"Woah, hold up a second, Mike. I never said anything about you killing anybody. What about you, Ted?" he asked as he turned to McFweed next to him. "You say anything about our mayor here killing anyone?"

"No, Sir. I hadn't mentioned that at all. But now that you ask, Mr. Morris, did you by any chance kill either of these two people? It would make our jobs a whole lot easier if you said you did."

"Jesus, no! I could never kill anybody, especially over something as petty as a stolen wallet," Morris screamed back at the accusation.

"So the wallet *was* stolen, then?" The PC asked with a smirk on his face. It seemed like they thought they had finally gotten him to slip up."

"What? No!" Morris exclaimed as he shrunk into the back of the chair behind him.

"Well, which is it? Did you lose it or was it stolen from you?" McFweed asked.

"To be honest, I don't know," the mayor said in a barely audible voice. It appeared from our side of the window that he knew he was cooked. "I had it at the restaurant, but it was gone when I went to bed. You know how busy Foggy Bottom gets on a Saturday night. Maybe it got stolen while we were waiting for our cab. I have no idea. You have to believe me, Russ."

"The only thing I believe in are facts, Mike. You lost your wallet, which was found next to a dead lady the day after you lost it. Then the very next day, another body turns up dead in the exact same place, with almost identical gunshot wounds, and this fella just so happened to have left fingerprints on the very same wallet that you say you lost."

"I hate to say it, but it sounds pretty clear to me, Mike," the PC lowered his head, shaking it in disapproval for what he was about to say. "We'll go over some questions with Kelly in a few minutes, but the facts are pointing to you, my friend. We've got no other suspects, and the press is begging us for answers. I do apologize for this, but my hands are tied."

With guilt in his eyes, Commissioner Blades stood from the table, faced his friend and continued; "Now if you can do me a favor, please stand up, face the wall, and place your hands on your head with your fingers interlaced so Lieutenant McFweed can put these cuffs on you. Michael R. Morris, you are under arrest for the murders of Jane Doe and Kenneth Webb."

The commissioner didn't even stay in the room to see McFweed cuff his friend. I opened the door and rushed out into the hallway after him. I saw him leaning up against the wall, one foot on the ground as his other one was planted directly on the wall, staring into the depths of the floor as though fighting back tears. I felt it was probably better to leave him alone, so I went back into the room with Jack and Diamond.

The mayor hung his head down straight in front of him. I couldn't see the tears, but could hear the sound of his sobs coming through the speakers in the other room. If I felt sorry for him before, I don't know what you would call it now. There was a pain in the bottom of my gut that I couldn't quite place. I can't say whether or not Jack and I would've gotten to the same conclusion as the PC did, but what I do know is, he had a hard job to do, and I didn't envy him for it. There was no going back from this now for him. Once he placed those cuffs on his dear old friend, that relationship was lost forever.

McFweed helped the mayor back into his seat while he left the room. That was our cue to exit the viewing room and meet up with the other two officers in the hallway. Even though I had hoped we would get a shot at the mayor's wife earlier, I was now secretly hoping that the commissioner and McFweed would take the helm on that interview as well. I guess there's a difference between being the one to bring a perp to tears yourself, and being a bystander as somebody else does that part for you.

Out in the hallway, the commissioner seemed to have regained his composure. The five of us stood in silence outside of the interrogation room, waiting awkwardly for someone to speak up and take control of the situation.

I, for one, was willing to wait out the silence for as long as it took. I was in no hurry to get into the other interview room and get back to work on the mayor's wife. I had seen enough tears for one day. I didn't think I had the composure to deal with a wife who just found out they arrested her husband for murder.

"What do we do now?" Jack asked, breaking the silence.

"You and Denver can knock off for the night if you want," the PC said as he looked at me and Jack. I'm going to have a conversation with Mrs. Morris in private. I think it would be best if none of you were around to witness it. Let her save some sort of decency tonight. Life is about to get real hard for her."

"Thank you, Sir. Keep us in the loop, please," Jack said to the boss as he nodded to me, letting me know there wasn't anything more we could say to change the man's mind.

I didn't think I was ready to call it a night just yet, but orders are orders. I followed Jack back to our desks, and grabbed my jacket. I was half tempted to ask him if he wanted to grab a burger before heading home, but I figured after the day he'd had, it was probably best to let him get on home.

Chapter Sixteen

The light switched on, piercing his retinas. The blindfold that had once been tightly secured around his face had finally sagged, drenched with three days of sweat.

A face rounded the corner–one that was all too familiar to him. What was once the source of such comfort and joy, had become the source of mortal dread.

As for the voice–that once comforting, now sickly sweet voice–it haunted his thoughts, and terrorized his waking moments.

"For what once was three, will now become none. Time to say goodbye, my dear boy."

He never even felt the impact of the bullets. He only knew the relief of finality and silence as his body went limp, and his life slipped away.

I made a pit stop at a liquor store on my way back to Union Station. Even though I wasn't feeling like I should celebrate the close of the case, or even that I needed a drink at the moment, I peeled open the lid and took a healthy swig off of the bottle, anyway.

The familiar burn that hit the back of my throat seemed to bring me the warmth and comfort of a crackling fire on a cold winter's night. It also brought me some much needed energy. I was feeling pretty down about things after watching the mayor weep in that interview room. Whatever it was, I felt like I was in no hurry to get home.

There was a twenty-four hour joint around the corner from the precinct that I had stopped into before on my way to catch the train after my shift. Not the greatest company around this time of the night, but I wasn't really in the mood for much chatter anyway. Something wasn't right, but I couldn't figure out what it was yet.

As soon as the dame behind the counter took my order, I looked to my left and saw the last person I wanted to see: Sarah. She was about four seats down from me at the other end of the bar. Her elbows were on the counter, and she seemed to be lost in whatever it was she was reading in front of her.

She must've felt my eyes burning into her, because she looked my way before I could turn my head back the other direction, and caught me staring at her. When I looked over again, she was coming my way.

"I never got the chance to apologize for how I left you that night, Max," she said. Which caught me off guard. "To be honest, I was embarrassed. Embarrassed by you, but even more so, embarrassed by my own actions. I handled that about as poorly as a person could. So, I'm sorry."

I didn't know what to say. I was flabbergasted. So I said the first thing that came to mind. "Listen, Sarah. I'm the one who should be apologizing to you."

"You're damn right you should be," she replied with a laugh. "You were such a gentleman for the first part of the evening, but then it was like a switch flipped in your brain, and you turned into an asshole out of nowhere."

"I know. It was a hard time for me, as you know. I'm not making excuses, but that's the truth. I wasn't ready for all of that yet, and instead of being honest with you, I got blotto, and the rest is history."

"Well, I just wanted to say to you that I was sorry. I figured you didn't want me to bring it up in front of the guys at work. So, I'm sorry, Max."

"Yeah, me too."

"I guess I should go. I'll see you around," she said as she gave the brim of my fedora a playful tug before she got up and left the diner.

I felt a huge weight leave my body as I watched her walk out that door. Knowing that she still had some sort of feelings for me made me feel less awkward, but more confused about the whole situation. I had always thought of her as the one that got away. But now, I had no idea what to think.

I thought about taking a stroll through Penn Quarter after I left the diner to see what I could see there. I still had the nagging feeling in my gut telling me we didn't have the right guy. No matter how much the evidence of the wallet pointed toward the mayor, it seemed to be too easy. The more I thought about it, the more inconsistencies came to mind.

Why would he dump the bodies right there for everyone to see? He, of all people, would have enough of his own people at his disposal to get rid of the bodies in a way that they wouldn't have been found so easily. Laying them in the alley seemed more like a statement to me. I guess he *was* running for re-election on the platform of cleaning up the city. But besides that, this made no sense to me. Displaying two dead people in an alley was not the way to get that point across.

And why would he use them tattered old blankets? Once again, he would have had the means to dispose of the bodies. Hell, he could've even rolled them down the banks of the Potomac from his own backyard if he wanted to. There was absolutely no reason for a man of his stature to leave the bodies out in the open if he were actually the one who had killed them. Especially not with his wallet being left at the scene, too. No, this was all an elaborate hoax, made for us to think it was the mayor who did this. *But who did it then? And for what reason?*

Those questions were at the forefront of my mind as I walked and drank and procrastinated my way through town, taking the longest way possible to get to the train depot. I would've had plenty of time to think and drink on the train, yet I just couldn't force myself to get there. There was something fishy about all of this, and going home now wouldn't get me any closer to finding out what it was.

Through my mindless wandering, I found myself right outside the front steps of the precinct again. Bottle in hand and fresh glaze over my eyes, I stumbled up the steps and walked in through the front door. Probably not the best decision I have ever made, especially not with the PC still there. I gave McFweed a wave as I walked past the front desk and into the locker room.

Now would be as good of a time as any to bury my new bottle in my locker at least. I sat in front of the lockers for at least twenty minutes, just thinking and staring at the walls. The blankets and the mystery person were still giving me fits. Not much I could do about it now, though, especially since Jack had gone home already. But I knew if I went home now too, I'd be awake all night thinking about it. Might as well do my thinking here. That way I'd already be at work if something came to me, and not stuck forty-five minutes away on the other side of the river.

I took another large pull off of my bottle before locking it up with the rest of my things in my locker, and laid my head down on somebody's bag on the bench. I must've been out within minutes, because when Diamond barged in and woke me up, I looked at my watch and it was already past midnight. I had been out for hours.

"Denver!" He shouted, appearing out of nowhere. "Get up! McFweed needs us back in the alley."

I rolled over from my resting position and placed my two feet on the ground. As I tried to stand, I lost my balance and fell face first into the lockers.

It wasn't my proudest moment. As I regained my composure, I asked, "What the hell is McFweed even still doing here?"

"We got a call about an hour ago. They found another body in that same alley. He wants me to take you over there with me to check it out."

"Okay," I said, not really hearing what the kid was saying to me.

"Are you okay, Sir? Do you need me to help you walk out to the car?"

"No, I'm good. I just needed a minute. My body doesn't work the same anymore. One of them things that happens when you get old, I guess," I said to him, not wanting to tell him it was because I was well past blotto at the moment. "Now, what were you saying before? And where were we going?" I was definitely still feeling groggy. I probably was in no shape to be going anywhere in an official capacity, but I followed the youngster out into the hallway and outside into the cold.

"The Federal Triangle, Sir," he explained as we walked to the lot that they kept the cars in. "Another body turned up."

"What?" I asked, still not really sure what was happening.

"We got a call a little bit ago about another body being found in that same alley as the last two days. You and I are going to check it out right now. Are you sure you're okay? I already told you all this back inside."

"Don't worry about me kid, I've been on this job since before you learned how to use the toilet by yourself. I'll be just fine. You worry about yourself."

He did the driving, which was probably a good idea, as I was still having trouble seeing straight. I opened my window so the cold air could help knock some sense back into me as we drove. I was slowly getting my mind around what was happening, though I still don't think I was fully up to speed just yet.

"Wait, so you're telling me they found another body in the same spot as before?" I asked, making sure I heard correctly what he told me a few minutes prior.

"Yes. A third body has turned up. And from the sound of things, it's from the same killer. Four shots to the chest, covered in a ratty old blanket, underneath the dumpster."

"Sounds like I was right all along then," I said aloud, but more to myself than to Diamond.

"Right about what?" The kid asked.

"Well, if the mayor was the killer, how'd he pull off this third shooting while he was behind bars?"

"That's an excellent point, sir," Diamond said.

"And stop calling me sir, kid. My name is Denver. Or Max. I ain't your superior, and you don't have to treat me like some god damned idol. Okay?"

"Yes, Sir. I mean, Denver, Sir."

I rattled him, I could tell. And it probably didn't help matters that I was three sheets to the wind at the moment, either. Here he was trying to make a good impression, and I was treating him like a recruit fresh out of the academy. Well, he's going to have to get his feet wet somehow. This isn't patrol. Ain't nobody going to hold his hand through the job at this rank. He'd just have to learn to grow thicker skin.

We pulled up to the alley a few minutes later. The yellow crime scene was taped up for the third day in a row, but for the first time since Sunday, the body was still lying on the pavement when we arrived. There was a small pool of blood that seemed to be coming from underneath the body. That told me that the wounds were fresh. I still felt like this place was used as a dump, both metaphorically and physically, and that the shooting was done elsewhere. There would've been a lot more blood if this guy had been killed right here.

That would also explain the lack of shells found at any of the scenes. So whoever is behind this has to have a vehicle that is big enough to not only transport the body, but also with enough room for the killer to climb in there with the body to wrap it up tight enough to make sure there isn't a blood trail when they dump it. So, that means we're looking for either a van or a truck with a bed. I laughed to myself, shaking my head. Yet more clues that we have no way of tying to any specific person.

"Does the PC know about this new body yet?" I asked, wondering if they had cut the mayor loose or not yet.

"I'm not really sure," Diamond answered, "But if McFweed knew about this, then I'm sure he relayed the message on to the commissioner."

"Well why don't you get on the horn and find out for sure, while I take a look at things over here?"

There was something sobering about sleuthing around a crime scene that had me feeling more like myself. I shook my head at Diamond"s greenness as I watched him walk back to the car to radio the lieutenant.

I'm sure he will make a good detective some day. He follows orders well enough, but I was stubborn, and wasn't ready to take him on as a partner just yet. Not when this was still me and Jack's case, and definitely not when there was still a killer on the loose.

Chapter Seventeen

I walked the same scene for the third time in three days, and didn't
notice much of anything new. The only two major differences
were the fact that there was a different blanket covering the body this
time, and the fact that there was no new outline around this particular
body yet. Like the day before, this body was laid right in the middle of
the two other chalk outlines.

I took a pen out of my pocket and used it to lift the blanket up so
I could see the victim's face. Black male, probably thirty to thirty-five
years of age.

It was a familiar face, but I couldn't quite place it. I crept down the
body, first taking a look at the chest wounds. From the naked eye, they
looked to be very similar to those of the other two bodies. We would
have to wait until the ME got a look at him to determine just how close
in proximity they actually were to the others, though. I continued
down the body until I came to the rear pockets of the man's pants, but
I didn't find any wallet on him. Which made me think to look in the
dumpster, just in case that had been tossed there in like the mayor's
was.

"Diamond," I shouted over to the car, "bring back a flashlight, will
ya? I wanna take a look inside the can."

"Sure thing, Max," he shouted back, leaving the sir part out this time.

The first victim was left with the wallet as a clue. The second victim was the person whose prints were left on that wallet. I was wondering what clue they would leave behind with this body. As far as I knew, the press hadn't yet learned that we had brought the mayor in for questioning, so I wondered if there would be more clues that pointed at him.

Thank god I'm not involved in talking to the press, I thought to myself. This seemed like it would be a nightmare to try to explain away. I felt for the PC. He probably lost his friend and his dignity over this case all in one fell swoop. Poor guy. But that's life behind the badge, I guess. Your friends are only your friends as long as you let them get away with breaking the law. Once the shield gets in between that, they're gone as fast as a mouse with a cat chasing after it.

Once Diamond returned with the flashlight, I opened up the lid and started digging around. Nothing stood out to me–it just looked like normal trash in there. Still, I would have the officers haul it in so me and Jack could have a better look at it tomorrow. Unless Diamond was feeling frisky, that is. If he wanted to sift through it, I wouldn't stop him.

That face though. It stared up at me through lifeless eyes as if trying to tell me who had done this to him. I hardly ever forget a face, but in our line of work, there's too many faces that we run into on a daily basis to keep track of the names that go with them. Still, this guy was giving me the nagging feeling that I was missing something. Something big. But I couldn't figure out what yet.

I wasn't that familiar with the uniforms that were holding down the crime scene. It wasn't too often that I was out and about at this time of the morning. So I had Diamond give them the orders to start bagging the trash from inside the dumpster. I wanted to see how the youngster handled himself while giving orders to uniforms, seeing as he was getting a promotion.

I looked at my watch again and saw that it was already almost two in the morning. I didn't think there was much left for us to do here, so I started back for the car, hoping the kid would follow my lead. It would probably be another hour or so before someone could get a hold of Sarah to come draw another outline and take her photos, and then another hour after that until the ME could come along and bag and tag the body.

Diamond showed up a few minutes later.

"Where to now, Max?" He asked as he stuck the keys into the ignition and fired up the engine.

"Back to the station. I still gotta get back across the river and get some shuteye in before I have to be back for my shift tomorrow. But let's take a slow drive around the block first, just to see if anything catches our eye."

"What are we looking for?"

"For starters, any vans or trucks that look to be out of place," I explained to him. "And also, we got a call about a person walking around this area late at night the last few nights. They walk with a limp, wear a hood, and may or may not have a gun on them. We was gonna be setting up a stakeout here and in Penn Quarter tonight looking for them, but that got set aside once they placed the mayor under arrest. So might as well take a look around while we're out here now."

"You're the boss, Max. Wherever you want to go, I'll take you."

"Would you knock it off with that boss shit? I already told you, I ain't your superior. Hell, I ain't even your partner. I'm just a fellow detective, working the same case as you for the time being," I said, as my anger started to return. I didn't know why it was bothering me so much, but it was starting to aggravate me like nothing else.

Diamond didn't say anything in return to that. In fact, he didn't say another word the whole time we were out looking around the neighborhood. Unfortunately, the pass around the neighborhood didn't net us any leads. In fact, we didn't see one truck, van, or person out at that hour of the morning. So we returned to the precinct, deciding to make another go of it the next day.

It wasn't until we pulled back into the parking lot at the precinct that he finally opened his mouth, and all he said then was, "Have a good night, sir. I'll see you tomorrow." His silence was enough of a message to let me know that he'd understood what I was saying. Normally I would take a swig or two off of my flask, but I was ready to be home and in bed by then. I tipped my fedora, and headed off for Union Station. Tomorrow was going to be a long day, and I needed time to think.

Chapter Eighteen

B y the time I finally walked through the front door of my house, it was already quarter to four in the morning. I passed up my nightcap and went straight to bed.

I tossed and turned for what seemed like hours. That was the worst part about getting close on a case—no matter how tired your body felt, tuning out your mind was next to impossible.

Three bodies in three days, all left in the same spot. The evidence pointed at the mayor, but I knew now that that was all meant to fool us—to keep us busy while the actual killer slipped through our fingers.

There had to be something we were missing—but what? I rolled out of bed and got dressed. Maybe creating a visual aid would help me organize my scattered thoughts.

I went to my kitchen table and pulled out a few pieces of paper and a pen from a drawer out of my filing cabinet, setting up seven piles in front of me. One for each dead body, one for the mayor, one for the evidence we had recovered, one for the witnesses we had questioned, and the last one I left blank for the moment. That would be where I would write down the link between everything else.

Jack never understood this way of doing things, said I was wasting my time by writing things out, but more often than not, it helped me. If I mentally walked through each crime scene again, I was sure that I'd come up with something. Something that I could take back to work with me and show to Jack and McFweed. Something we could set out on first thing when we all arrived at the station later on.

I started with the first body. That page was called **Jane Doe**. I went over what we knew first. White female, no ID, most likely a prostitute, four shots to the chest from close range, no spent shells found anywhere near the body. She'd been covered in the knit blanket with the corner missing from it, and had been seen in the area recently–even talking to the kids playing stickball, possibly. But neither Clarence nor John had mentioned anything about recognizing her. Could she possibly be a case of mistaken identity? I put a big question mark on my page about that. No spent shells found anywhere near the body.

I moved on to the next victim. **Kenneth "Spida" Webb**. Four shots to the chest from close range, just like the first; no spent shells were found in the area, just like the first. Had been involved in the Penn Quarter Boys gang. Arrested not too long ago for busting out a storefront window and taking a necklace for one of his girls. Known for being a minor pimp in the neighborhood. His prints were on the lost wallet of the mayor that was placed in the dumpster above the body of Jane Doe, and he was covered in the other half of the knit blanket that Jane Doe was found under.

Could this be an inside job? Were the Penn Quarter Boys doing a bit of policing in their own gang? I put a big question mark about that on the page. That was something I would definitely revisit. This sounded like a very possible lead for us to look into further.

The third page I titled: **John Doe**. Black male, possibly thirty to thirty-five years of age. No ID, though I did recognize the face, and was found covered in a knit blanket different from that of the other two bodies. Four shots to the chest from close range, and again, no spent shells were found in the area. They found no evidence on or around the body that pointed to the other two murders or the mayor, except that he was also covered in a blanket and left at the same place.

I wrote a note to check the blankets handy work. Maybe they were knitted by the same person? With nothing else to go on, I left the rest of his page blank.

Fourth page was titled: **Mayor Morris**. Michael R. Morris was brought in for questioning after they found his wallet at the first crime scene. Was subsequently arrested for the murders of both Jane Doe and Kenneth Webb. Was in Foggy Bottom on Saturday night with his wife at a restaurant for dinner. Took a cab back to Georgetown after dinner. Doesn't know where he lost his wallet, but says maybe it was stolen while awaiting a cab ride in FB. Is running for re-election on the platform of cleaning up the city's crime rates.

Could this be why he was targeted as the fall guy? If I could find out why he was getting the blame for this, then I could figure out who was really behind the murders. I wrote down three large exclamation points on that page, as I felt this could be one of the keys to unlocking the case.

On the fifth page, titled: **Witnesses/Suspects**, I jotted down each person we had spoken to since Sunday afternoon:

John and Clarence were the biggest ones. They seemed like a nice family to me. The mother said she had seen girls like Jane Doe walking in the area and talking to the kids while they played ball.

Could Jane Doe be one of these women? We never showed the mother a picture of the victim, but I made a note for me and Jack to do that first thing the next day. We needed to get a read on her reaction to the photos of the crime scene. Father was not around for questioning, and we didn't ask about him.

The mother had complained to her son that she hurt her hip the night before at work, though. We will have to get her occupation when we go for a second interview. Could she be the limping figure? Might be a wild goose chase, but I felt it was worth looking into. You never know what odd bits of information could lead to breakthrough on a case.

Michael and Kelly Morris. Mayor of DC and his wife. I stated everything we asked him on his page. We never personally got to speak with his wife.

And then there was Marie Anglin. The woman who found Webb's body while walking her dog. She had refused to answer the door when we stopped by. Unknown age, unknown if she walks with a limp. I secretly hoped she wasn't the key to the case. She seemed a tough fish to pin down.

The sixth page was for the **Evidence Recovered**. Two half blankets, a corner piece of blanket, the mayor's wallet, and a second blanket, uncut.

Did the second blanket being left intact mean that the killer was done killing? Or was the last killing done so hastily the killer wasn't as prepared as he'd been for the first two? I placed two giant question marks on that sheet of paper. The wallet seemed to be less and less of a clue the more that I thought about it. It was more of a tool to get us on the scent of the mayor. Maybe it was found on Kenneth Webb and thrown into the trash for the main purpose of giving us a suspect to chase after. The hunch loomed large in my mind, yet unshakable as I continued my notes.

I read and reread every piece of paper that I had written several times before I moved on to the blank page: **Links.** The three things that seemed to be in common on all three of the bodies were the mayor, the bullet groupings, and the blankets. I knew the mayor was off the hook for these killings after John Doe had turned up dead while Morris was in custody. And we already knew the same person killed all three victims. Which brought me back to the blankets.

So I wrote **BLANKETS** in big bold letters on that page and nothing else. That was what we needed to focus our attention on. That was what was going to solve this case.

By the time I had finished writing and going over everything, it was damn near eight in the morning. I took the pages with me and placed them on the coffee table in front of my couch. If I was going to get any sleep at all, it would have to be right now. My alarm clock was set to go off at ten, so I could afford a two-hour nap. Luckily, plotting those notes put me more at ease, and before I knew it, I was asleep.

Chapter Nineteen

The phone woke me up about an hour and a half after I fell asleep on the couch. I stubbed my toe on the corner of the coffee table as I stumbled to get it, and let out a yowl that could've been heard from two blocks away.

"Yeah?" I barked into the phone's receiver. I didn't do well on no sleep, especially not when I was also woken up before my alarm clock went off. "Who's there?"

"Hey, Max, this is Frank down at the morgue. I just wanted to let you know what I found in the pants pocket of the latest victim you guys found last night."

"I went through those pockets myself, Frankie," I told him. "There wasn't nothing in them."

"This seemed to be stuffed pretty tight into his front pocket. It could've been easily missed unless you got real deep in there. Anyway, it was one of those political flyers you see hanging from all the telephone poles around town. But they crumpled it up pretty tight, barely the size of a shooting marble."

"Okay, so, that's it?" I asked him. Hardly seemed like an instance to be calling a fella at this hour of the morning.

"Not really," he said as he continued, "it's one of those flyers about cleaning up the city. You know, the ones with the mayor's face plastered front and center? 'Cept someone took a marker to his face and crossed out his eyes to make it look like he was dead. With all that's gone on over the past few nights, I figured you should probably take a look at this pretty darn quick."

"Yeah, sure sounds like it. Did you give Jack a call yet? He's got a car, so he can get to you faster. I'm stuck all the way out here in Virginia. It will take me at least an hour before I can get into town."

"Yep. Already called. He said he was gonna be over after a shake. Just wanted to give you the heads up, too."

"I appreciate that, Frank. You need us to stop back by and take a look at the body after I get in?"

"I doubt it. It's early enough in the day that I should have the reports to you by five. It's a lot of the same. Four shots to the chest, all in close proximity. Someone has definitely been excelling at their target practice."

"Sounds good to me. You know how much that place creeps me out. Okay, I'll talk to you later then, Frank," I said as I hung the receiver back into its cradle on the wall.

I rushed to grab a fresh set of clothes so I could jump in the shower, still feeling the effects of exhaustion, not to mention my toe still smarted. A little cold water would wake me up in no time. I grabbed my bottle on the way into the bathroom so I could have a little breakfast before I brushed my teeth, too. I was going to need something to kick my ass into gear.

The second I turned the water on in the shower, I heard a loud thumping at the door. I peeked through the peephole to see Jack's smiling mug looking back at me.

"Morning, Jack," I opened the door to let him in, "I was about to hop in the shower, but you're more than welcome to come in and wait.

You can make yourself some coffee if you want. The pot is clean and there's filters and grounds in the cupboard above the sink."

"I think I'm alright. But hurry up, Frank has something for us down at the morgue. Some sort of flier with a messed up picture of the mayor on it," he explained.

"He just called to let me know. Let me just shower, and then we can be on our way.."

"Get to it then. And when you're done, I wanna recap of what went down last night."

I walked him into the living room and showed him my pile of paper that I wrote my notes on last night and told him to have a look. It would probably still need a lot of explaining, but it should at least catch him up to speed with where I was at. I left him to look it over while I hopped in the shower.

I smelled coffee as I was drying myself off. I normally saved that for my days off, but I could definitely use a cup this morning.

We went over each sheet of paper that was on the coffee table one by one. Jack had little to add, except he agreed with me that we should look into the Penn Quarter Boys a bit more to see where that took us. Despite his support, I couldn't shake the feeling that we were still missing something–something that was right under our noses. It bothered me, but I couldn't seem to put my finger on it, no matter how hard I tried.

We drove to the morgue and looked at the flier that Frank had wanted to show us. The picture had exes drawn over the mayor's eyes, and there was some writing that covered his face that read, "NO MORE."

Someone was clearly trying to frame the mayor. But with how badly crumpled up it was, we wouldn't be able to pull any prints off of it. Just another clue that led to another dead end.

"Somebody had it out for our mayor, looks like," I said as I held the flier in my hands. "But at least now we know for sure that he was being targeted. Still, something doesn't add up to me."

"Whatcha mean, Maxey?" Jack asked.

"I can't put my finger on it, Jackie Boy, but I can't help but feel we're missing whatever it is that links this all together. I think we need to go back to the alley and start again: Canvas the area in the daylight, and go back to each witness and talk to them again. My bet is we've already encountered the killer. We just need to find that missing piece that ties everything together."

"What are you suggesting?" Jack asked.

"We need to find where these people were killed. Find that, and the rest will be easy."

Chapter Twenty

*T*he showroom bell rang.

    "Shit!" exclaimed the killer, shrouded in shadow, bloody rag in hand. Someone had entered the factory.

    Things were moving too fast. Way too fast. Despite all her planning, all her hard work, all her care in ensuring they would pursue the mayor instead of her. Her meticulousness had all been for nothing. They were already here.

    Well, she didn't let it happen before, and she wouldn't let it happen now. Grabbing the brass knuckles, she crept behind the door and waited in the silence.

    She had been through too much for too long. She'd defended her life once, and she'd do it again.

    They were coming for her—she could sense it. And when they got to her, she'd be ready for them.

I radioed Davis to have him and Miller meet us back at the crime scene again. We were going to need all hands on deck for this mission.

McFweed and Diamond were right behind us as we led the way over from the precinct. With six of us out canvassing, we could each go in a separate direction and cover more ground than if it were just the two of us.

The two uniformed officers met up with us a few minutes after the four of us had arrived at the alley. After deciding who would go where, we set out on our mission.

We sent Davis and Miller down to 14th street and told them to take a left and have a look down Constitution, while we sent McFweed and Diamond over toward Pennsylvania down to 12th. Me and Jack were going to head up 14th to G before we hung a right and came back down 13th to Pennsylvania. With our game plan in action, all three groups set off on foot.

The funny thing about all of this was, we had all been in and around this neighborhood several times over the past three days. But how many times do you pass a work truck or van on a daily basis and think nothing of it? Dozens, maybe. But now that we knew what to look for, you'd bet your ass that we were going to check out every last one we came across, writing down makes, colors and license plate numbers while doing so.

As me and Jack came to the crosswalk at Pennsylvania, I noticed something that I hadn't seen over the course of the past three days: A textile factory. High on the red brick walls was a faded and weather chipped painting with the name of the company: Brown's Blankets, written above their logo, and a ball of multicolored yarn with two tapestry needles crossed behind it. I was amazed I hadn't noticed it before–you couldn't miss it if you tried.

"Would you get a look at that, Jackie Boy," I said while pointing directly to the building across the street from us, "I think we might need to do some blanket shopping. Whatcha think?"

"I'm game. It *has* been getting colder out recently. The fire just isn't keeping these old bones as warm as it used to," he said with a smirk on his face.

We crossed the street and headed directly for the front door to the storefront. A little bell above the door jingled as we entered the small room. There were blankets hung from every corner of the room, with price tags attached to each one. One blanket in particular stuck out to me immediately. It hung directly behind the counter, front and center–an ash gray number with little black spirals knitted throughout. It was a dead ringer for the blanket that was cut in two and draped over victims one and two in the alley. Jack gave me a look to let me know that he saw it, too.

Me and Jack looked around and perused the small showroom as we waited for someone to come and help us. This took a lot longer than expected. The room was no bigger than ten by fifteen feet, but judging by the factory's exterior, the factory expanded far beyond this small shop. The bell above the door wasn't heard by the workers in the back.

A few more minutes passed, and still no one. I rang the bell on the counter multiple times, to no avail. We tried to listen for any sounds of production in a back room, but heard nothing at all from where we were standing. Running low on patience, Jack nodded at me and let me know he was going to peek his head around the corner behind the front counter of the store. I reached for both my badge and my weapon. Jack had his gun drawn as well as he crept around the corner with his back upright against the wall, only allowing his neck to move while the rest of his body stayed as stiff as a board.

It was quiet as a cemetery as we neared the door to the back room. Light came from a small window on the door to illuminate the hallway, but there was still no sign of any workers present. The hairs on the back of my neck were standing up, and my heart started beating in double time.

Jack stopped short of the door and gave me a look to stay behind him. He slid his back up against the door to get a look into the room beyond. I could only see a long wooden table with work stations from where I was standing. There was still no movement or noise coming from the other side of the door.

Jack moved his hand to the doorknob and gave it a twist, slowly pushing the door open with his back. All the while his gun was in his right hand, finger resting on the outside of the trigger along the bottom of the length of the barrel. I moved quietly past and slowly went ahead of him, looking both ways as I crossed through the frame of the door.

It was anticlimactic. The place looked empty–like everybody had stopped, gotten up, and left the building for some unknown reason. I could see now that there were two more tables of the same size as the one I had seen through the window.

"Where'd everybody go?" I asked Jack in a tone barely more audible than a whisper.

"Beats me, but we had better keep it quiet still. Don't know if they left or if they's hiding. You go to the left, and I'll go right. Then we'll meet back in the middle."

I started off to the left, as quietly as I might. I still had my gun straight out in front of me. As big as this room was, there wasn't much to it besides those tables in the middle of the floor, and some shelves and cabinets bordering those. I was walking away from the lights in the center of the room, and it was getting darker with each step I took. So dark, in fact, that I looked behind me to see if the lights were even still on. I was so far in the back, I could barely even see them.

Unsure of my footing, I began to tap each step to make sure there were no obstacles in my path. Holstering my weapon, I began to use my hand to feel my way.

I found the wall I'd been hugging earlier, and planted my back up against it as I crept sideways. I could've easily just turned around and met back up with Jack, but something inside me told me to keep going. I would eventually run out of both wall and darkness, I told myself. Something inside me needed to see what was at the end of the tunnel.

Slowly but surely, I made my way all the way to the end of the wall. There was definitely something there—I could feel it! I wondered what, if anything, I was missing in the darkness around me.

Was the killer watching me as I crept right by him? I didn't know, and I wasn't sure I wanted to find out. Wherever I'd ended up, I felt like I was watching one of those monster movies from my youth—gave me the heebie jeebies like no one's business. So much for investigating—now I just wanted to get back to Jack as soon as possible. As I repositioned myself to hug the wall going in the other direction, my foot got caught up in something slick, and I instantly fell, hitting my head on cold concrete, and passing out like a rock.

I have no idea how long I was out. It could've been two seconds; it could've been a day. I hoped it was only a few minutes as I began to come to.

"Maxey!" I heard Jack yell in the distance.

A specific smell played on my nostrils. My addled brain couldn't place it at first, but then of course the realization dawned on me. Once you smell it, you'll never be able to ignore it again. The unmistakable, irrevocable, unforgettable, sickly-sweet, metallic scent of blood.

Finally awake enough to muster a reply, I called out with what strength I had. "Yeah, Jackie Boy, I'm over here. Far back corner of the room."

"Get over here, there's something yous gotta see," he shouted back.

Still disoriented, I stood back up and began to stumble towards the sound of his voice. My back was cold from the dampness of the floor, and as I neared the light in the center of the room again, I glanced down at myself.

Everything, from my shoes, to my favorite pants, to my new shirt, to my hands, was completely covered in blood.

Chapter Twenty-One

"Maxey!" Jack exclaimed as he looked up. "What in the hell happened to you? Are you hurt? Did you get into it with somebody?"

"No" I replied, still dazed. "I got tripped up on some plastic on the floor or something, maybe a tarp even. Knocked me out cold. When I came to, I smelled blood."

"I think you found something back there, Maxey. But whose blood, do you think?"

"I don't know. I don't think it's mine. I didn't see or hear anybody when I was over there," I explained. "Maybe that's where the killer did them. Only explanation I got to be caked in this much blood. It must be pooled on the floor. I bet when we get some lights in here, we'll see that this was some sort of torture chamber."

"I gots something for you to see first, then let's get the hell out of here and call for backup. This place is giving me the creeps. I don't have a good feeling about any of this at all."

"Me either, Jackie Boy," I agreed, "Show me what you gots for me to see."

Jack waved his hand for me to follow him as he led me back to the side of the building that he had checked out. My body seemed to be having convulsions as I followed him. It was more than nerves. I think it was my detective's intuition kicking into overdrive. We were close, I knew that, but I could also sense an impending doom, it seemed. The quicker we got the hell out of this building, the better.

"When I was looking over here, I came across a desk tucked into the back corner of the room," he said as he was walking. "My guess is it's the boss's desk. It's got magazines and catalogs and pictures of bedding and blankets all over the top of it. But that's not what I wanted to show you."

"Well, what is it then?" I asked. I couldn't make anything out on the desk yet. Nothing looked out of place to me from my vantage point. There definitely wasn't any blood on or around it, at least not that I could see.

"Just come look," he said, not giving away any clues at all to me.

I kept following him until I was right up next to the desk. He wasn't joking about the amount of bedding and linen catalogs placed on it. There were two sets of small cabinets with open slots on the top of the desk at each side, which were both full of papers. The left one read **Invoices**, while the right one read **Orders**. I still didn't see anything that looked to be a clue, so I asked, "What gives, Jackie Boy? It looks just how you explained it. I don't see what's gotten you so jazzed up about it."

"Then you had better have a look-see at this," he said as he picked up a framed photograph from the center of the desk and handed it to me. It had been hidden from my view between the two sets of filing slots.

"Well, I'll be a monkey's uncle, Barnaby," I said with a flabbergasted chuckle. I finally remembered where I'd seen the third victim before. "You gotta be shittin' me, right?"

"How long you know me now, Maxey? And how many times I ever pulled your leg like this? I can't make this stuff up. It's all right there, just sitting here waiting for us to find it," he replied with his own smirk and laugh. "Ask me, I think this puts a nice bow and ribbon on things."

I stood with my mouth gaped open as I stared at the family photograph. "Seems like it, Jackie Boy. I think Mrs. Brown has some explaining to do."

"She sure does. Come on, Maxey. We better get outta here before somebody else shows up. We ain't got no backup with us. We're in prime position to be ambushed."

"I agree," I seconded, "we gotta get back to the alley and get on the horn to McFweed. He can radio in some more squad cars to at least put this place on lockdown for us."

We both drew our weapons once again as we headed back towards the entry to the showroom. The whole place was still quiet–too quiet, if you ask me. I got the sense that we were being watched, though I had no idea how. The warehouse portion of the building didn't seem to have an upstairs to it, but there were plenty of air ducts that ran the length of the ceiling. I shivered, and did my best to shake the feeling off.

We walked with determination–what good would it be knowing who the killer was if we weren't able to make it out of the building and make an arrest?

But neither of us was prepared for what came next. I only had a split second to react, but Jack never saw it coming at all. Poor guy didn't stand a chance.

Chapter Twenty-Two

It was a long and frantic run for me. I tried to pick up my partner, simultaneously dodging the barrage of Mrs. Brown's fists. There would be no surviving this stuck in these close quarters–we had to find a way to get some space between us. My head was throbbing, and I hated to think what might happen if we didn't escape soon.

She had ambushed us, alright. She had been laying in wait behind the showroom door–Jack had walked us right into her trap. By the time I saw the glimmer of light reflected off her wedding ring, it was already too late–she had already dealt the knockout blow to Jack.

I shoved right past her, crossing the threshold of the doorway, and making it into the showroom, knocking her to the ground. We were only a few steps away from the front door now, but her determination told me she would not let us go so easily.

She grasped at Jack's left leg, and the jolt nearly made me drop him. I tugged one last time, harder than I had before, and managed to free his ankle from her grip, as the two of us tumbled onto the floor.

His full weight landed on my stomach, and I gasped, struggling to breathe. With my back to the front door, I reached into the inside of my jacket and felt the familiar coolness of my revolver in its holster. I knew what I had to do, and I knew I would only have one shot.

In one fluid motion, I raised my weapon and fired.

She had stopped crawling towards us, so I made our escape. I reached up with my left hand and pulled down on the handle of the door, opening it up behind me.

After tugging on Jackie Boy for several minutes, I finally managed to lug him all the way out onto the sidewalk with me. By this time, there was quite a crowd gathering. Having gotten us to safety, I collapsed, lay flat on my back and focused on breathing. The fresh air was intoxicating, and euphoria came over me as my strength returned with every inhale. Off in the distance, I could hear sirens wailing.

After a while, I registered the relative silence within the factory, and began to wonder about Mrs. Brown. Had my bullet found its mark? I pushed myself up on my elbows and looked around. The crowd was still there, but they were beginning to back off. I flashed my badge to them to let them know I was a copper..

I got up onto my knees and got really close to Jack's face so I could listen to his breathing. It was fluid. Didn't sound like he was straining, so I took his face in the palms of my hands, rubbed his cheeks a few times, then hit him with an open palmed slap.

There was still no movement from Jack, so I wound up and slapped him again, this time with the back of my hand. Just as the "smack" was reverberating into the crowd, I heard a voice behind me shout, "Denver, what the hell are you doing?"

I turned my head to see McFweed and Diamond running towards us. The sirens sounded like they were about to turn down our street.

"It's about time you got here," I said as I looked up at McFweed. "Ain't we a sorry bunch?"

"We got cars coming. Somebody will take a look at yous two. But first, what's going on in there?" He asked as he pointed to the front door. "Who's in there?"

I gave him the rundown of what had happened inside, beginning with Mrs. Brown. How she was the killer, and kept coming after us until the very end. I told him how I'd fired a round towards her, and that the second that I'd seen a chance to get us out of there, I had.

I told him about the blood in the back corner of the building, and about the tarp that I had tripped over. I told him about the blankets in the showroom, and about the one that was a dead ringer for the one found at the crime scene. I told him about the photograph that we found of Mr. and Mrs. Brown with their two sons, Clarence Jr. and John, on a camping trip to Lake Fairfax. I told him how in that photo Mrs. Brown held a hunting rifle and a blue ribbon for marksmanship.

I told him everything I knew, and everything he needed to know to close the case.

And after I had told him all of that, I realized that now, for me at least, it was finally over.

Really over.

Jack was safe.

The mayor would be released.

Mrs. Brown would be brought to justice.

We had done an amazing job, and everything was going to be ok.

For now, however, it was definitely time for a drink.

Chapter Twenty-Three

M e and Jack were given the rest of the week off to heal from our injuries. Jack's jaw was broken, and he suffered some pretty bad facial bruises and scrapes. I rode with him in the cab home from the hospital after he had his jaw fixed up. After I got him settled into bed, I realized it wouldn't be right to just leave him all alone. So I bedded up on his couch for the rest of the week. I was up every morning, noon and night, grinding up his food so he was able to ingest it through his wired-up jaw.

I think it was good for us, to be honest. It was just the two of us with nothing to do except keep each other company while we healed. It gave us a chance to remember what was really important, as well as to talk through some things. We were able to hash out most of our differences, and he lectured me plenty about my drinking, which I took in stride. I knew he was right, but damned if I didn't want to knock him in his broken jaw while he was talking about it. By Sunday, I had made it three days without a drink, and I had the shakes something fierce. But the time together was good for us–especially since he told me he was turning in his badge once this was all over.

Meanwhile, the case was still constantly on my mind. I couldn't believe how everything had turned out. It was my hunch that had brought us back to the streets that day. It was also my hunch that had pointed us to the textile factory.

Forgotten details began to come to mind as I began to piece everything together. I remembered the cane that I had seen by the front door when we first questioned Mrs. Brown and her two boys that first day, and the strange look she had given to both of them when they first made mention of the blanket. Deep down, I had known something was amiss there. *Had she been the limping figure spotted around the alley as well?* It started to add up in my mind as I pieced the facts together.

Not only had my intuition brought us to her in the first place, but it was my gun that had brought her down. I sighed with satisfaction. I couldn't remember the last time I'd had to discharge a firearm. Honestly, I was amazed by all that had happened in the last 72 hours. No matter what happened from this point forward, I knew I had done my part.

There's nothing worse than being sidelined, though, especially when there was still work to be done. We had the who, sure, but we didn't yet have the why. I knew that was driving 'Ol Jackie Boy crazy. It definitely was for me. I couldn't wait to get in there after our week off, and give Mrs. Brown hell. She might've been able to fool everyone else, but Jack and I had caught her, fair and square. And now, just as soon as we were able, we were gonna dig our talons into her, and make sure she told us everything.

Chapter Twenty-Four

J ack's telephone rang on early Sunday morning, rousing me from a sound sleep on the sofa.

It was McFweed, alerting us that Colleen Brown was alive, and finally awake. I was a little disappointed that my shot hadn't killed her, but the folks upstairs needed her alive so they could piece the whole damn thing together.

"Jack," I said, tapping him on the shoulder as I walked into his bedroom. "Wake up. McFweed wants us at the station. Colleen Brown woke up, and we need to get over to the hospital to question her."

"Well, which is it? The station, or the hospital?" He asked grumpily, wiping the sleep from his eyes.

"He told me the station. He didn't know that I had been bunking over here this week, said he was glad he didn't need to make two phone calls."

"What's he doing there so early?" Jack asked as he checked his watch, seeing it was only twenty minutes after eight in the morning.

"Dunno, but he sounded pretty urgent. I didn't question him."

Jack was moving better now, but not well enough to do anything quickly, and not yet competently enough to drive. I hoped he'd be able to get down to the station with me in a timely manner. We didn't know how much of a window we'd have to speak with Mrs. Brown. If we were going to get answers, we needed to get them now.

I grabbed his car keys, and helped him down the stairs, boosting him up into the cab of his '48 F-1 pickup truck. Hopping into the driver's seat, I took off for the station.

McFweed and Diamond were waiting for us at the lieutenant's desk when we finally walked through the front door, excited to touch base before heading to the hospital. Neither said anything, but I could tell what they were thinking when they saw Jack. Not only was his face still bruised up, but his movements were only slightly better than that of someone's bed-ridden grandpa.

"Denver, hang back a second," McFweed said to me as Diamond and Jack headed back out. "How's Jack? You think he's up for this?"

I nodded. All of us were rattled by Jack's appearance, but I still had faith in him. "If you'd asked me that question an hour ago, I'd say no, not in a million years. But something woke him up on the ride over here. Maybe it was getting back to work–I dunno. But he's as ready now as he's ever been. Don't let his appearance fool you–he may be a touch slower than usual, but he's ready to go. No question about that."

"Thanks, Denver. That's all I needed to hear. You ride with Diamond, I'll drive Barnaby over. I've got something I need to run by him."

Cole Diamond already had the engine cranked over and was waiting for me as McFweed and I walked down the steps toward the street. I felt a little red in the face as I opened the door to get in. Last time the two of us were in a car together, I was more than a little drunk, and I felt I needed to apologize for that. As soon as I slammed the door shut behind me, I started to say, "hey, listen kid," but was interrupted.

"I don't think we got off on the right foot the other night, Max," he said, taking the words right out of my mouth. "So I'd like to pretend that this is our first day of working together so we can get past that mess a few nights ago. Deal?"

"Deal," I answered. "So I'm sure you got the news then, right?"

"About us? About me and you becoming partners since Barnaby is stepping down?" He asked.

"That's it. You okay with this move?"

"I'm plenty okay with it, on one condition."

"Sure," I said, shaking my head at the rookie's audacity. "Go ahead. What is your one condition?"

"That the first time I see you as messed up as you were the other night when we worked together, I go straight up the ladder and ask for a new assignment."

I didn't answer him right away. I couldn't believe he'd even thrown those terms on the table. The kid had balls, no doubt about that.

"You got yourself a deal, kid. As of right now, I'm three days sober. Will I make it four? I've got no idea. What I do know is that I've taken it too far and I need to ease up on it. I'll make an effort to dial it back–and that starts with getting rid of the bottle that's in my locker."

"You don't need to worry about that. McFweed already took that out. As well as all the other bottles of booze that were stashed around the precinct."

Stunned, I didn't answer. I didn't need to. If McFweed knew about my problem, I knew I had changes to make–especially if I wasn't going to have my trusty security blanket, Jack, with me anymore. Slowly, I nodded my head. "I'll do my best to do better, kid," I said. "You deserve it, I deserve it–and hell–the precinct deserves it. I don't want to retire in 20 years and have this be my legacy. So, I guess that means I'd better start changing now. I know it takes some nerve to talk that way to your superior, but I just want to say–thanks. I know you're saying it for my own good, and I aim to do something about it, and be a better man."

Diamond nodded. "Thanks, Max. I have faith in you. I may not let you get away with it like Jack did, but let me know if you ever need support. I'm your partner now, and I'd like us to work as a team."

"Sounds good, kid. Sounds good." I smiled as we drove off. Things were definitely going to be different with a partner like Diamond, but he was a good kid, and I couldn't help but feel that maybe this particular change would be for the better.

Chapter Twenty-Five

A nurse was waiting outside the front entrance when we arrived. Evidently McFweed had phoned ahead and told them that we were on our way. She greeted us kindly, and asked us to follow her to room 109, where Mrs. Brown was recovering.

Two uniformed coppers stood at attention on either side of Mrs. Brown's hospital room, keeping an eye on things. I didn't recognize them, but nodded at them as we approached, letting them know I acknowledged them for their work guarding our perp. McFweed stepped aside, letting me and Jack go into the room first.

Mrs. Brown looked to be in pretty bad shape. Her eyes looked like they weren't able to focus on anything. She lay flat on her back, her left wrist handcuffed to the railing of the bed. She called out, "who's there?" when we entered the room, her voice was barely audible over the constant whir and hum of all of the life support machines. A slow drip from an IV bag ran down its tube and into her right hand.

"This is Detectives Denver, and Barnaby." I told her. "Do you remember us?" I'm sure she knew exactly who we were, but if I let my anger show at all, we would lose our shot at questioning her. I know from the look on Jack's face that he was having a hard time. This woman had knocked him out cold, and now, he had a mouth full of metal wires holding his fractured jaw in place.

"Yes, I remember you two. You were the ones who were trespassing on my property."

"We were there, yes. But trespassing might be a little harsh. We were actually there conducting a search...as I'm sure you know...when you blindsided us."

Mrs. Brown ignored the insinuation, and continued on, nonplussed. "I was well within my rights of the law. I was protecting my family and my property."

"Well, I guess we'll have to agree to disagree on that, then," Jack mumbled through his mouth full of wires.

"What was that? I can't quite understand you. Could you open your mouth a bit more when you speak?" Sitting up, she smirked, observing her handy work in Jack's mouth. Given her current state, I was surprised she had the energy to mock anyone. I was almost impressed by the layers of evil Mrs. Brown continued to demonstrate.

"Cute," I said. "Can we please stick to the matter at hand, Mrs. Brown?"

Suddenly distracted, Mrs. Brown began to look around, suddenly interested in more beside Jack's jaw. "Where are my two boys?" she asked. "Can they come and see me? I'd really like to see my two boys now," she said, as concern seemed to wash over her all of a sudden.

"I'm not exactly sure," I said. Which was a lie of course. "My partner and I have been out of work all week. But I can ask the lieutenant, if you'd like."

"Yes, I would like that. They're the only family I have left," she said as she started weeping silently.

"Speaking of family," Jack chimed in, taking charge once more, "why'd you kill your husband, Mrs. Brown? Hell, why'd you kill any of them? That's the part we're having a hard time piecing together. The blankets tie this all back to you and your warehouse, and our colleagues told us that they recovered a gun and some .45 caliber ammunition from your house as well. We know that you were the one that pulled the trigger on all three of them. But in all honesty, we'd really just like to know why you did it. What's your husband have to do with all of this? And why'd you try to frame the mayor?"

"Why?" She asked, caught off guard by the question, and clearly not fully present. Her expression wandered in and out of the present moment, until finally she responded with an aggressive, "Why should I even give you that satisfaction? Why don't I have you talk to my lawyer instead?"

"You're right," I nodded, looking down at the floor as I scratched my head. "you don't have to give us anything." I decided to try a tactic that had been successful before for me. "We have enough evidence to put you away as it stands now, and you *could* wait for your lawyer to get here. You can stay as quiet as you'd like that way."

I looked up and made eye contact with her, making sure she was hearing what I was saying, and considering every word. "But what does that show your two boys? What does that tell them about their mother? That she's a coward? Is that how you want them to go through the rest of their lives thinking about you? That when the time came to put everything on the line, when the time came for you to help put everything together and confess for your sins, you clammed up and hid behind a lawyer? What message does that send your boys? What sort of example does that set for them to follow when they're grown and they have to learn to make hard decisions?"

Flipping the script and making a perp think of the wake of destruction that they've left behind, and the long path to forgiveness for their loved ones to navigate, often brought about a change of heart. If there was any compassion at all left inside Colleen, then I hoped this tactic would work.

She gave us a hundred yard stare, carefully plotting out in her mind what she was going to say next. After thinking hard for several uncomfortable seconds, she finally spoke. "If I tell you everything, will you bring my boys here to see me?" Jack and I gave each other a look before responding.

"I'll see what I can do," Jack added. "But I'll tell you this much. You keep quiet, and the odds of them coming here go down exponentially."

"Okay," Colleen, considering everything carefully, in a slow, deliberate manner, "if it means I can see my boys, I'll talk,"

"Good choice," I said.

Unfortunately, our battle wasn't over. Colleen was a slippery fish. After several more awkward moments of her staring into space and gritting her teeth, her demeanor changed once more.

"I think I've changed my mind," she stated with conviction, puffing her chest and flashing a charming smile. "I wanna see my boys first. Bring me my boys, and then I'll talk," she concluded, and reached for the glass of water on her bedside table, taking a refreshing drink as she began to relax again.

"That's not really how this works, Mrs. Brown," I said, adding a little matter-of-fact tone to my voice. "Now, if you want, we can turn ourselves back around and walk right back out that door. No sweat off our backs—we already got you. Look down at your hand that's cuffed to the bedpost. You think you have any cards at all left to play? No. You're cooked. So right now, the only thing you have to contemplate is whether or not you want to see your sons again before we try you for murder."

I gave Jack the nod and we turned and headed for the door, acting like we were done with her. As my hand reached the doorknob, I heard a crash and felt a shower of cold liquid spray my face. She had thrown the pitcher of water that had been on her bedside table.

Seeing that there was nothing else within her arms reach that could do any damage to us, I said mockingly, "So, I'm hearing you don't want to see your kids. Is that right?"

Her rage sent chills down my spine. I'd never seen a perp quite this out of control before. Her anger was palpable, even from across the room. "You shut your goddamn mouth!" she shouted, "You don't know nothing about me. You have no idea what I'm capable of."

She was right. We had zero clue what to expect next from her. She had already blindsided us twice. Even though she was cuffed to the bed, I wouldn't put it past her to break her own wrist, if it meant getting free to come after us.

"See?" said Jack, none too pleased with the events that had just transpired. "That is exactly how to do things to ensure that you never get to see your boys again, Colleen. We are the ones in charge, not you. If you want any chance at all of seeing them ever again, I suggest that you talk to us."

I walked right up and got in her face. "What's it gonna be, Colleen," I doubled down. "Are you gonna see your kids again, or not?"

She lunged at me and I jumped back. She was fuming now.

"Keep it up, Colleen," Jack shouted. He was trying his best to keep his cool, but he was losing that battle. "One more outburst like that, and I'll slap cuffs on your other wrist and both of your ankles too. Now you gonna talk to us, or are we wasting our time?"

"I should've killed you both when I had the chance," she snarled, as saliva sprayed my face. "You're both lucky my gun was back home when you broke into the warehouse. I wouldn't have hesitated to put bullets in both of you. You two think you're smarter than me, don't you?"

"Whether we are or we ain't don't matter," Jack spat back, seeming to lose interest in playing her game. "If you ever want the chance to see your boys again, it would be in your best interest to start singing our tune. Can you get that through that thick skull of yours, Colleen?"

Her head started to spin. She wasn't used to not calling the shots. I braced myself for another outburst, but just as quickly as her rage had come on, it ebbed away. Energy draining out of her, she sank into the mattress, defeated. Her hands covered her face as the sounds of sobbing filled the air.

"I loved him," she moaned through the sounds of sniffles and cries. "I truly loved him. What was I supposed to do? I gave him my life, and he treated me with the respect of one of those whores he was paid to protect." She broke down sobbing after that last part, looking up at the both of us through tear soaked eyes.

I gave Jack a look. We both knew we had finally broken her. I sat on the edge of the bed and put my arm around the woman, comforting her. "It's gonna be okay, Colleen," I told her.

Silence filled the room for a few minutes as her inner battle continued. If a face were a book, hers would be one in extra large print, as the expressions she was conveying told us exactly what was going through her brain as she weighed both the pros and cons of confessing. Ultimately, confession won. She looked up at the two of us at last and said, "Okay, I'm ready."

"Go ahead, ma'am, we're listening," I said back to her as I looked at Jack, giving him the go ahead to grab his notebook from his pocket and get ready to take notes.

"I guess I should start at the beginning, then" she finally continued, tears rolling down her cheeks. Her voice was shaky as she tried her best to regain her composure. "I met my husband through a mutual friend 10 years ago, and he asked me out right away. Clarence was a true gentleman when we first started dating. He brought me roses at least once a week. But as soon as we bought that house and moved in together, things began to change. He started staying out late, and drinking more than he should. There were strange phone calls at strange hours, and continued assurance that everything was fine, and not to worry my head about it.

"Then one night, probably about a year ago, I was closing up down at the warehouse, and it was Clarence's night to spend with the boys. As I was locking up, one of your men came 'round and let me know that Clarence had been picked up for selling drugs on one of the corners up in Penn Quarter.

I had known about his past. Clarence used to run with those boys. I had hoped and prayed he would never go back to that life...." She reached for her hankie that was on the table, wiping her eyes dry before she continued.

"He ended up doing a two week stint in jail," she said with a shake of her head, bringing her frustration to the forefront. "I was fuming mad. I actually had the locks changed, but when I saw the look on my boys' faces as he was pounding down the door, trying to get in, I couldn't stand my ground anymore. I cared about my boys too much." Her eyes seemed to stare at the wall behind us as she spoke of her children.

Sighing deeply, she continued, "Things didn't change though. He was missing dinner more and more frequently, and deep down, I knew where he was. I just knew."

It seemed to be all coming together now, just as I figured. "Is that why you dragged the mayor into all of this then? A little payback for your husband being a victim of his 'Cleaning Up the Streets' campaign?" I asked.

She mumbled something under her breath as she shot me a look, continuing on as best she could despite the interruption.

"The more Clarence missed supper, the more suspicious I got. So I went to the warehouse one night to see what he was up to." This seemed to hit a sore spot for her, as her face contorted into one of fright. "On my way there, I saw him necking with some pretty, young, white girl in the alley." She clenched her jaw tight, grinding her teeth. "I just about lost it right there on the spot." Her eyes flicked between the two of us for a few moments before settling solely on Jack, willing him to feel the same pain she'd felt that night.

"I'll be honest. If I'd had the gun on me then, I'd probably have shot the both of them right there on the spot. But instead, I rushed home, vowing to get revenge." She paused again, this time coughing violently, her emotions overcoming her.

Taking a few moments to regain composure, she finally continued, "A few more weeks went by, and he was still up to his usual shenanigans. But, all of a sudden, he was starting to bring gifts for the boys. I think he was trying to get me back on his good side and not raise suspicion, but it had the opposite effect.

This recollection brought a new look from her, one we hadn't seen before. Gone was the emotional wreck who murdered her husband, and from her shell emerged a savvy and respectable businesswoman.

"I did the books for our business, and I'll tell you this much—we weren't bringing in the kind of money it would take for the weekly splurges he was making. So I asked around. I knew some of the people in the neighborhood who had their ears to the streets."

Another pause—probably for dramatic effect. Colleen reached for the glass of water that was on the side table next to her bed. She slowly took a few sips off of the glass, licked her lips to get some moisture back in them, and restarted with a glint in her eye. "Turned out, just as I had suspected, Clarence had taken a new role with the Penn Quarter Boys. He was overseeing this young kid named Spida, who was running girls in the neighborhood."

She took one more drink of the water before dabbing her lips of the excess and placing the glass back on the table. "I had seen Spida around, and he was no good at all. You could tell just by looking at him. Clarence was the money man. But not only that, he was also the muscle for the girls. And low and behold, that same girl I had seen him necking with in the alley, was one of the girls he was supposed to be protecting."

It was all starting to make sense to me now. Colleen Brown was not only a woman scorned, out to take revenge on her lowlife husband, but also a woman who never made a move without a calculated plan ahead of time. Which made me ask to myself—what were the other two victims to her? Were they just collateral damage? Were they just in the wrong place at the wrong time? There were still gaps in Colleen's story I couldn't quite understand.

"That's a nice little picture you're painting about being the victim and all, Mrs. Brown," Jack interjected, "but you still haven't answered any of our questions yet."

This only elicited a sly grin, as she looked Jack dead in the eyes, but continued to ignore him. "The last straw was when me and Clarence were out for dinner in Foggy Bottom last Saturday night." Her eyes suddenly shone with glee as she relived the swanky experience. "I was still mad as all hell, but if he was going to treat me to a fine night out with that whoring money, I was going to take full advantage of it." She paused again, smacking her dried lips, almost like she was tasting the meal all over again. "And it was good too. Best meal we ever had. The night was going so good that I almost forgot I was mad at him at all." She laughed gleefully at the memory, but her smile quickly evaporated into a scowl as she continued.

"But then that slodge Spida showed up as we were waiting for our cab. Bragging about how he picked a wallet back in the restaurant."

She clenched her fists as her eyes shot daggers. "And that was it. That put me so far over the edge that I knew I was going to kill him."

"Couldn't you just take the boys and leave? What good did putting the three of them down bring to anyone?" Jack asked.

She sat up in bed, giving Jack another glare. "I played nice the rest of the way home, and as soon as we got back, I went straight to bed. Yet unbeknownst to Clarence, I had a plan."

"A few minutes after I was in bed, I heard the front door open." Her eyes grew wide with excitement as she unfolded her plan. "That's when I got up, reached into the nightstand next to the bed, and grabbed our gun. I followed Clarence as he led me to our warehouse, of all places. I didn't care where it was–I was putting a bullet in him." She laughed, reaching for another sip of water.

"Turns out, he was there to meet Spida to collect money. And Spida had that blonde whore with him too." Her voice emphasized the word "whore" like a pastor emphasizes the word "devil."

"That was just a bonus for me at that point. I waited until all three of them went inside before I followed." She was boasting now, her maniacal laughter filling the room. "I pulled the hood from my sweater down around my face so they couldn't recognize me. They obviously thought they were alone. I wish you could've seen the look on Clarence's face when I pulled back my hood. He looked like he'd seen a ghost!" Her laughter continued as her face glowed with joy.

She inhaled deeply, her raucous laughter quieting to a snicker. "I don't even remember what I said, but whatever it was, it worked. Soon after that, without even realizing I had done it, they were all tied up. I took one last glance at my handiwork, took a few steps back, and pulled the trigger.

"Eight shots in all. Four into Spida, and four into the girl. They were both dead instantly. But Clarence? I waited on that one. I didn't want to kill him right away. I wanted him to be scared–and suffer, too.

"I went back outside, to our large garbage bay, and took one of our blankets that we couldn't sell out of the dumpster. I brought it back inside and cut it down the middle. I untied the two bodies and covered them in the blankets. That's when I saw the wallet that Spida had stolen lying on the floor next to his dead body. It was convenient–I figured I could use that to frame whoever it was for the murder. When I looked at the ID, I could hardly contain myself. It was the perfect plan–as though God himself had dropped it into my hands. If it weren't for the mayor and his anti drug policy, I wouldn't have been so hellbent on killing Clarence in the first place. It couldn't have worked out any better." Satisfied, she titled the glass of water all the way to the ceiling as she drank the last of its contents in one large gulp. "And that, boys, is how you commit the perfect crime."

"Boy," Jack said. "You really put a lot of thought into this, didn't you?"

"There was no way I was gonna let that man poison my kids' minds with his drug-selling ways." This brought another round of the maniacal laughter we had heard before. It lasted a few minutes before it sputtered out and she continued, straight faced, with, "He had to go."

I was at a loss for words with what I had just heard, as well as her complete lack of sympathy for her victims. I still had a few questions, though. "How'd you get the bodies to the alley?" I asked. "You couldn't have drug them there yourself. And there was no trail of blood, either. So how'd you do it?"

"Linen cart." She said, with such arrogance that I felt stupid for not thinking of it before. "Nine o'clock on a Saturday is pretty quiet around these parts. Either everyone is home, or they're out in some other part of town living it up. I flung that whore into the cart and wheeled her over to the alley. Getting her out was a chore, but I got it done. Left her right under the dumpster like the trash that she was." Her face lit up with a smile as she recalled her own brilliance. "That's when I came up with the idea that I would leave them all in the same place. And to complete the ruse, I tossed the mayor's wallet into the dumpster so it would be found next to the body."

"So what role, if any, did the blankets actually play in all of this?" I asked. It has been the one thing that I never figured out yet throughout all of this.

"Nothing. Not really," she answered with another laugh. "You cops are all the same, aren't you? Not *everything* has to have some diabolical reasoning behind it. I had blankets galore in the warehouse, and I needed something to cover the bodies with in case I ran into someone during transport. Nothing more than that. They were just accessible when I needed them,"

Jack and I looked at each other and shrugged. She wasn't wrong. It was in our pedigree to look at everything as a possible clue.

She shot us both another glare, signaling that she wasn't quite finished yet. "I hurt my leg while I was dumping the girl, so it was an even harder struggle the next two nights." Her face once again shown that the ordeal had been difficult for her. "But with ambition comes strength." I shook my head at the depths of her insanity, as she flip-flopped back and forth between business strategist, and psychopath.

Her bravado shifted to remorse as she shared with us the final moments of her husband's life. The same man that she claimed to love, not even ten minutes ago. "I waited until Tuesday night to kill Clarence. I left him tethered up to that beam for two whole days." Her lips pressed hard against one another. It was easy to see how hard this part of it was on her. "He pissed and shit himself and was whimpering like a puppy who got left behind in the house while everyone else was outside having fun." With the hard part over, she regained her poise and looked at the two of us with conviction before adding, "but he needed to know that I meant business."

Pain flashed across her face as she recalled the very last moment of his life. "I didn't even say anything meaningful to him before I pulled the trigger. I just walked in, took aim, and fired four shots into his chest. I slaughtered him like the worthless animal that he was." She paused again, a brief sigh escaping her lips. "And have never felt so free."

A creepy grin crept onto her face as she said the words aloud. The grin turned into laughter as she confessed, "it was the most liberating experience of my life."

I didn't know about Jack, but I definitely needed a minute to take all of that in. I looked over at my partner, and he just shook his head back at me. We'd had some doozies over the years, but I can't remember one that could even come close to what we had just heard Colleen Brown tell us. She looked to be at ease though. Getting all of that off of her chest probably felt good.

But we weren't here to sympathize with the woman. She was, after all, a cold blooded killer. It was time for us to wrap things up now that we had our confession. But first, I had a little bit of justice of my own to administer.

"You know what, Mrs. Brown? I asked.

"What's that?" she asked.

"If you had just had enough strength to kill and move all three of the bodies on that first night, you probably would've gotten away with all of this. We had already placed the mayor under arrest before the third body was even discovered."

Laughter filled the room once more as she shrugged her shoulders and said, "Well, you can't win 'em all, I guess. I'm not sorry for what I did." She paused again, as if realizing something all of a sudden. "If you really think about it, I cleaned up the city more in those three days than the mayor has in his whole term. I'm leaving this city in better shape for my boys than he ever could." She smiled at that, thinking she had done us a favor or something. "I can't wait to see those two faces. When are you going to bring them in?"

"You actually think you did the city a favor don't you?" Jack asked her. "You do know there are laws against vigilantes in the District, don't you?" Jack raised an eyebrow, giving her time to consider the consequences of her actions.

Just as he saw her open her mouth to reply, he said, "Oh yeah, and one more thing. About those two boys of yours," Jack added with as much of a smirk that he could muster with his mouth messed up with wires, "Your mother came and picked them up a few days ago. They're back in Dover with her. And from what we've heard, she ain't ever bringing them around you again."

Chapter Twenty-Six

Enraged cries and wails followed us all the way down the hospital hall, and into the foyer. The four of us eyed each other, trying our best to stifle laughter, as we walked towards the main entrance of the hospital. Confession in hand, our job was finally over.

"Get everything you needed?" McFweed asked as we joined back up with him and Diamond out in the hallway.

"Yes, Sir. We sure did." I replied as I followed them back out to the parking lot.

I drove Jack back to his house and helped him inside. He still wasn't feeling his best, and asked if I could stay with him for a couple of nights.

I agreed. I knew I wasn't going to be seeing too much of the guy from here on out. Sure, maybe I'd stop by from time to time to check on him, or maybe he'd make an appearance down at the station to say hi to the fellas, but that would probably be it. A Christmas card, maybe even a birthday card, but I can't see us getting together to share a cup of coffee every week or anything like that. We were partners, not friends.

He must have been sensing the same thing as me, as his eyes started to well up with moisture. He retreated to the bedroom, stating he needed to grab some sheets and blankets so he could make up the couch for me.

He was losing his livelihood. I had to remember that. Come Monday morning, I would return to work, same as usual. But for him, he was going to have to learn a new way of life. I felt for the guy.

When he returned with the bedding, I asked if I could have some privacy for a few minutes to make a phone call. He obliged and retired back to his bedroom.

For as long as I had been a detective, I had always celebrated a close with a drink. But this time was different. With Jack gone and me sober, I decided to do something different. So I walked into the kitchen and dialed a phone number. Somehow, I knew it by heart, even though I'd only ever dialed it a few times. As the phone rang, my heart began to race.

"Hello?" I heard the woman answer on the other end of the line.

"Hi, Sarah, it's me, Max. I was wondering if you'd like to give us another chance? Think I could take you out for dinner sometime this week?"

"Hi, Max. I think I'd like that. I've been wanting to go to this place downtown for a while called The Colony. It's on DeSales. Have you heard of it? They have entertainment in their lounge, so we can have a drink before dinner."

"That sounds great. Also, to let you know, I'm drying out. Or trying to at least. How does Wednesday night sound? Say 8:00?"

"Sounds perfect. I'll see you then. And, Max. Thanks for the phone call. I appreciate it."

As I hung up the phone, the smile on my face reached from ear to ear. Thank god Jack was in the other room—I don't think I'd ever hear the end of it if he saw me this giddy. *Here's to new beginnings,* I said aloud to myself, somehow already feeling like a new man.

If this past week had taught me anything, it's that you couldn't take life for granted. I knew I had to start making every moment count–both at work and in my personal life.

Monday morning was going to be the start of a new life for me. New partner, new girl, and new lease on life.

I didn't know what the future held. What I did know, was I was going to do my best to enjoy it.

I hope you enjoyed taking a peek into the world of Max Denver. This is the first book of what I hope will be many more in the future. If you enjoyed this book, it would mean the world to me if you would take a few minutes out of your day to leave a rate and review on Amazon. Ratings and reviews help self-published authors, like myself, sell more books and help each and every one of us grow that much closer to reaching our goals of becoming full time authors.

If you would like to receive updates about future books in the Max Denver series, and news in general about me and my writing, sign up for my mailing list at tylercraigauthor.comOr for any and all updates give me a follow on Facebook at Tyler Craig – Author.

This book is dedicated to the memory of the real life Teed McFweed.

First and foremost, I would like to give a huge thanks to my family. Without their support, I never would have been able to pursue this dream of mine of becoming an author. They have always supported me to their fullest ability, and it has not gone unnoticed.

I would also like to give a special thanks to my go-to guy, Marcus Callahan, for helping me with some of the law enforcement details throughout this book.

Also, thank you to Krislyn Lyon. Through a random Facebook comment came the best editor I have ever worked with. Hopefully there will be many more opportunities for us to work together in the future.

I also want to give a big thank you to Karly Bookheimer, Pete Martin, Leslie Mainer, Kassi Mackey, Randy Raush, Neil Hathaway, Jason Delanty, Dennis Delanty, Janice Delanty, David Voth, Amber Stafford, Jesse Zoller and Hailee Heckert.

Also, one last thank you to the person who told me that Max Denver "had no legs." Honestly, if those words were never spoken, this book probably wouldn't have been written.

Tyler Craig hails from the San Juan Island's in Washington State. Though he has spent most of his life in the desert region of Arizona, his Washington roots have never strayed. Tyler got his start in sports writing and blogging, having covered Seattle sports, national sports and sports betting. Though sports remain a major part of his life, creative writing has become a passion for him for the better part of two decades now as he focuses his writing goals towards storytelling. His love for Seattle sports, animals and his family are shown throughout his writing, having named many characters in his stories after them. For more on Tyler, head on over to tylercraigauthor.com.